BEHIND
THE
IRON DOOR

STEAMPUNK SHORT STORIES
by

BRAD R. COOK

THE BARONESS
TOUCH THE STARS
LAST FLIGHT OF THE MAJESTIC
A CLOCKWORK HEART
THE LEGEND OF SPRING-HEELED JACK

BONUS
MAN AT THE CROSSROADS

THE BARONESS
(written 2010, published 2021)
TOUCH THE STARS
(written 2016, published 2018)
LAST FLIGHT OF THE MAJESTIC
(written 2016, published 2017)
A CLOCKWORK HEART
(written 2011, published 2016)
THE LEGEND OF SPRING-HEELED JACK
(written 2019, published 2021)

BONUS
MAN AT THE CROSSROADS
(written 2003, published 2020)

All Covers Created by Brad R. Cook
Images are Creative Commons or used with permission.
Interior Layout by Brad R. Cook

For

The Dreamers

Each of these stories represents a step of my journey. Take steps toward your dreams, you never know where it will lead you.

Contents

Genevieve continues the family legacy, but tonight it is personal. The short story that inspired my trilogy, *The Iron Chronicles*.

Hobson Manning spent the last few summers helping Professor Teague build a rocketship with Mac and her ferret, Sprocket. Inspired by his favorite novel, and having watched the stars his whole life, Hobson is ready to depart. However, a few people fear this endeavor and will do anything to sabotage this journey.
Now he wants to touch the stars.

Opportunity and tragedy are two sides of the same coin. The only question, which one lands face up. Rex Fielder wants to be a big movie director. So, he sold everything he had to get on the maiden voyage of the world's first luxury airplane, The Majestic. Among the rich and famous passengers, he hopes to find something exciting to film, and prove to a studio he can make a movie. Now he only needs something worthy to capture. When the chips are down, sometimes bad luck can be the best luck of all.

"The greatest aviation disaster movie ever made."
– Rex Fielder, director

The Baroness

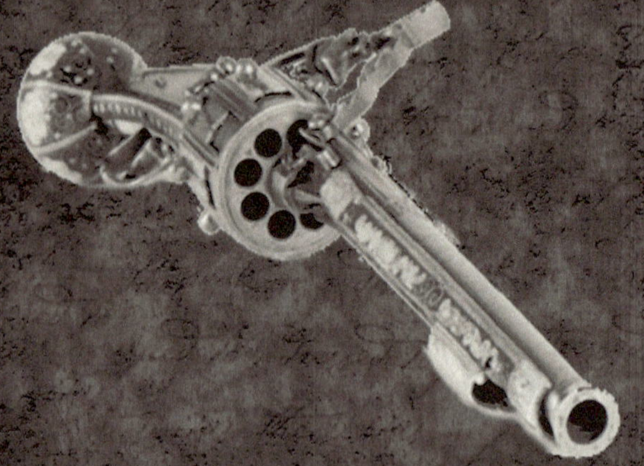

Brad R. Cook

a steampunk short story

The Baroness

a steampunk short story

London 1888

I crossed the hand-woven Indian rug, as firelight flickered off the silver locket that rolled around my fingers. My thoughts drifted to the night of my ninth birthday when mother gave me this gift. The locket hadn't left my neck in ten years, and though we rarely spoke – except when she'd scold me – I treasured the memory.

Tonight's attendance was mandatory. The Lord had been one of father's oldest friends, but these parties lost my favor years ago. They remained nothing more than a den of similarity. The same people engaging in the same conversations, week after week. The scenery barely changed from house to house as the party floated around the city in a schedule crafted years in advance. Struggling, I finally cut through the long-tailed tuxedoes and bejeweled corseted dresses, discovering sanctuary in an open space. The nobles, and the gilded world surrounding me, drop away as if I were the last leaf clinging to the tree in a fading autumn breeze.

A hand on my shoulder sent panic rippling through me, but the nasal accent accompanying caused my skin to crawl. "Baroness Kensington, a moment please."

"Lord Calhoun, how may I assist you this night?" I spun around, and the hem of my gown swayed above my boot, and showed just enough ankle to be scandalous.

"Join me for a tip of the glass, and maybe a summer along the Nile." The wiry gentleman demonstrated the water with his hands.

Still a slug trying to marry up. Unfortunately, I made the perfect target and had since childhood. To be polite I replied, "That's such an appealing offer. I don't know how I'll get over not having a drink in the desert."

Lord Calhoun rolled his eyes. With a pursed smirk he scanned the other ladies in the room. "It's your loss. I'm quite the catch."

"I'm certain you'll make some woman miserable."

He snapped his head around. "What was that?"

"I said I'll be miserable for not accepting such an offer."

"Yes, of course." He walked away with a puzzled expression.

I bit my lip to stifle a laugh and shook my head as he floated off. I stepped further from the crowd. Sanctuary lay on the balcony only a few feet away, but a woman in a lace gown suddenly blocked my path.

"Genevieve Kensington."

My hand rose to my heart, pressing the broach pin into my skin. "Mother."

"You should be more polite."

"You would say that about Lord Calhoun." I took a deep breath, but she said nothing. Her stoic gaze remained fixed on me. Hollow eyes stared back at me, at least some things never changed. "You've returned from the Sahara," I panned the room to avoid my mother's hardened expression. Once we'd shared a close bond, but now a shadow fell between us. Facing my mother I said, "You're a little late."

"I came back for you."

I cocked my head to the side. "Really?"

In a cold, aristocratic tone she commanded, "Come, I wish to speak with you."

"I was just leaving."

Her hollow eyes didn't flinch. "It is important I speak with you alone."

"Follow me out, if you must." I left knowing she'd be three steps behind just as decorum dictated. She'd always been a master of every societal rule. My heels tapped on the wooden floor echoing off the large empty hall. My gate never wavered and I didn't look back. I couldn't or I might lose my will.

Two servants, dressed in the white wigs and tight waistcoats of the previous century, pulled open the doors as I passed.

The cool night air rushed around me, filled with the sweet smell of rain and a hint of the stench from the river. Fog smothered the space between buildings and obscured the carriage house. The flickering orange glow of the gas lamps cast an eerie hue upon the cobblestone street but only illuminated the ever-thickening fog.

It had been a night just like this that my father returned from the Sahara. I still remembered running out to scream at the moon.

"Does it not please you to see me?" The voice came from behind, but I didn't answer. Slowly, I pulled off my gloves, and wrung them through my fingers.

My steamcarriage arrived at the base of a wide stone stairway. The finely decorated carriage had no horses hitched, but carried an intricate steam engine on the back that hummed along at an idle. A thin column of smoke rose from its stack.

Finn sat atop his perch, holding a small wheel that controlled an integrated column of gears connected to the steering hitch. I tried to dapper him up with the dark suit and floppy cap, but he insisted on a hunched posture and darting gaze like he still worked the docks.

The streetlamp behind the carriage wheels cast shadows of the spokes upon the misty veil that clung to the dampened cobblestones. My hand passed through the silken mist as I approached the carriage and I reached for the locket, gliding my fingers over the intricate design.

My mother had always cared, she might have never understood me, but she too treasured the good moments. She might run around the world on some adventure, but she always returned with a gift for my birthday.

Finn's eyes grew wide. Tufts of bright orange hair stuck out from underneath his hat which he tipped up. He started to jump down, but I stopped him by raising my hand.

My heels, clicking on the cobblestone, fell silent leaving an eerie stillness. The cold brass handle sent a chill through me as I opened the carriage door. I reached in and felt the smooth curves of the lacquered wood under the seat. Pressing the rose popped open a compartment. I reached in, and my fingers slipped around a silver-and-ivory handle lying on a velvet base.

"I thought Hell might try something tonight, but instead of frightening me, you've only angered me." I drew the flintlock revolver from its holster, spun on my heel, cocked back the hammer, and pulled the trigger. Smoke and fire exploded from the pistol.

My mother shattered like cathedral glass and the pieces disintegrated into dust.

The wind whipped the bits away. The ache in my heart plummeted deeper into my chest, and I struggled for the air to breathe. Remaining upright, I tried to inhale deeply, not an easy task in this corset. We hadn't finished our dance, and I wasn't about to let this demon slip away.

Finn shook his head. "Sure looked like your mum. Good lady she was. Your father was never quite the same when they both didn't return from Egypt."

"*That* was not my mother." Pulling the flintlock to half-cock, I quickly rotated the cylinder and locked it into place, getting the next shot ready to fire.

"Of course not." Finn grabbed his hat and wrung it through his hands.

"The iron and silver shot just shattered the demon's spectral façade. It didn't kill it."

Reaching back into the steamcarriage, I pulled out a set of multi-colored lens goggles. Once on, I adjusted the brass housing trying to find the right combination. I thought rotating the blue crystal lens into place would correct the spectral harmonics, but it took only a simple rotation of the rose quartz amplifiers. As the lenses aligned, the demon came into view, gripping its stomach as it writhed on the cobblestones. "Finn, did you make my father wait this long?"

"No, sorry ma'am. Coming." Finn leaped down with a long iron chain in his hand.

"There. The creature is trying to drag itself off." I pointed to an empty spot in the street. "Hurry, Finn, bind it with the chain."

"Yes, ma'am."

I guided Finn using the spectral viewer. As the iron chain wrapped around the demon's skin, it lashed out, writhing, struggling to break free as it twisted in agony. I allowed myself a slight smile. Hell and I had battled twice before, but this time felt personal. I'd faced mythical creatures since my father started to train me, but this doppelganger taunted me.

"Lock its hands in iron." I pointed at the cobblestones. "It's the only way to hold a demon."

"Trying milady." Finn kept the thrashing chain under control, but couldn't get the manacles on both ends around the demon's invisible hands.

The demon unleashed a screeching cry like a banshee's wail as it lashed out violently and hurled Finn against the carriage. It tore at the iron chain with teeth and claws but was unable to fling them away.

I raised the flintlock revolver but hesitated. My father's words ran through my mind. *When you fight the demons of Hell, don't lose yourself to the darkness.* I lowered the pistol and watched for an opening. As the demon pulled its arms in, to gather strength before another explosive outburst, I darted in and slapped the manacle around one of its wrists. The sound of iron slamming shut echoed down the foggy street like a cell door closing. I ducked under the demon's thrashing arms and secured the other manacle. The demon fell to the cobblestones.

I pulled off the goggles and handed them to Finn who returned to the carriage. He retrieved an ornate wooden box and held it out with the latch turned toward me. I stepped up and ran my finger over a brass plaque engraved with the initials M. K.

I paused. Thoughts of my parents stung like fresh cuts on my memory. I followed in their steps, continuing my family's long legacy as demon slayers. I accepted this burden, even embraced it, but I wanted to explore the world. I unlatched the lock and opened the case. The box was my father's, but the tools inside came from both my parents. With a few specialized pieces from the generations of Kensingtons who protected the crown from supernatural threats.

I retrieved a small silver box filled with white chalk from the cliffs of Dover. Shaking the powder from the corner, I formed a circle around the iron manacles hovering above the street. Reaching back into the box, I retrieved a small glass-and-gold vial of Holy Water from Templar Cathedral in London. Without pause or malice, I sprinkled the Holy Water over the demon and recited the prayer to send this creature of the old world back to the depths of Hell.

The demon became visible, like a fog swirling into form. The shattered face staring back belongs to my mother. Torn like a demonic shell, cracked flesh peeled back in a tight-lipped smirk. Sunken, haunted eyes peered through me. Every nerve fired within me. As if this demon's gaze seared my soul. The cobblestones tumbled inward as flames engulfed the demon. The creature burned to ash which was drawn underneath the street where the untouched cobblestones still smoldered.

I took a deep breath and stepped into the steamcarriage. With a flip, I open the locket into my palm, and stare at the photos of my parents.

The End

Touch the Stars
Brad R. Cook
A steampunk short story inspired by Verne

Touch the Stars

A Steampunk Fantasy Inspired by Verne

Long Island, New York, 1896

The Moon's rough edges came into focus as Hobson Manning adjusted the telescope's aperture knob. Shifting gray hues on the surface gleamed in the sunlight. Staring at another world, Hobson wondered what's its surface must be like to stand on. He'd read *From the Earth to the Moon* by Jules Verne every summer for a dozen years, maybe more. A smile crossed his lips, soon, he'd be going to the stars.

Hobson pushed away from the towering telescope. Hooking his feet and hands on the ladder's railing, he slid down from the viewing platform. Dropping onto the wooden floor with a thud rattled the whole workshop. Hoisting a large box on his shoulder, Hobson rushed through the door to the backyard.

Professor Teague stood over a copper canister, muttering pressure calculations to himself. The thin-framed man with wild, white hair that hadn't seen a comb in years, brushed his hand across his brow. Adding another smudge to his off-white suit.

"Ready to test the rocket?" Hobson asked. "Think it will make it to the Moon?" He set up a tripod and fixed the large wooden box to the top.

"What?" The professor popped up. His pupils were magnified by the lenses on his goggles. "No, this only has enough thrust to reach about… a thousand feet. I'm testing the nozzle's aperture."

Hobson tugged on his flat cap. "I'm ready to watch it soar through the sky." He opened the box, extending the lens and its accordion shroud. Sliding a glass plate into the back, he focused the lens and looked over the camera to ensure a good picture. "Hold there, and I'll take a photograph." The professor froze, holding his pose for several minutes until Hobson replaced the lens cap.

"I just need to set the fuse and we'll be ready for test twenty-four." Professor Teague pointed to the small wooden table. "Take notes, Master Manning. A three-quarters of an inch nozzle with thirteen grams of propellant."

"The propellant is Guncotton, smokeless powder?"
"Yes."

Hobson snatched up a pen and the professor's journal. He scribbled furiously, recording everything from the angle of the rocket, *eighty-eight degrees*, to the length of the fuse, *seven inches*, or approximately seven seconds. "Ready, professor."

"Excellent, good lad." Professor Teague pated his front pockets, then his back pants pocket, and finally checked inside his white suit coat. "Now where did I put those matches?"

Hobson scanned the tables and even the ground. The professor reached into one of his outer coat pockets and declared, "Ah-ha! Here they are."

The old man twisted off the cap of a small brass vile and pulled a wooden match from inside. Striking the head against the rough underside, he coaxed the flame to life and carried it to the fuse. Sparks erupted from the string and the professor rushed behind a brick wall he had erected near the fence. As Hobson grabbed the camera, the door opened and Ms. Rutter, the professor's housemaid stepped out with a tray of tea and finger sandwiches.

"Away Ms. Rutter!" The professor jumped out from behind the bricks.

Before anyone could take another step, the sparks rushed into the bottom of the copper tube, followed shortly by fire and smoke exploding out the nozzle. The rocket remained on the launch struts, as billowing smoke engulfed the backyard.

"Rocket test twenty-four—failure." Professor Teague waved his hands, coughing as he emerged from the cloud.

Hobson uncurled himself from the camera. Setting it down in the grass, he crossed out the last line he'd written in the journal. Exactly like the previous twenty-three attempts.

Tea dripped from Ms. Rutter's skirt and apron as finger sandwiches lay scattered in the grass. Slapping her hands down, she unleashed an exasperated sigh. "Well, I never…in a thousand years…I never."

"Do forgive me, Ms. Rutter." Professor Teague twisted one of the smoldering ends of his hair to snuff it out. "But we are conducting important research."

"I pray for you," she said as she bent down to pick up the sandwiches. "And I'm not fixing the sandwiches again."

"Apologies, I'll have Master Manning inform you of any future tests." The professor walked over to the smoldering remnants of the rocket, trying to brush away the smoke with his hand.

As Ms. Rutter charged inside with a huff, Hobson asked, "What happened to the rocket?"

Professor Teague's head rose out of the smoke. "The nozzle… too wide." He coughed. "All the propellant rushed out at once. Burned too quickly."

"Can you fix it?"

"Of course, I only need to funnel the nozzle more and shrink the aperture. The real problem is remixing the propellant."

They entered the professor's workshop and stepped up to a table lined with metal cylinders, and a mortar and pedestal encircled by spilled black powder. Two tables filled the rest of the room. One held a complex brass contraption with tubes coiled on one side and vents slats on the other. The other held a series of rolled-up plans, scraps of paper, and a pile of notebooks.

The shelves of Professor Teague's laboratory held exotic devices and inventions. Some conventional like the hair-drying hat, or steam-powered penny-farthing. Others Hobson couldn't figure out, like the chin press, or peanut re-sheller. Everywhere he turned, something ignited his imagination. None more so than the telescope rising out of the floor and poking through the roof.

Hobson walked over to the telescope as the professor checked his calculations on a large chalkboard filled with equations. The young man didn't ascend the stairs but looked up into the orange sky.

"I wonder what the stars look like up close?" He pulled off his cap as he leaned back. "Do you think we'll get close?"

"I'll be happy to make it into orbit," the professor muttered as he erased the last bit of numbers and letters on the board.

"I hope we pass the Moon?"

A clatter outside drew both men's attention. Hobson rushed over to the door with Professor Teague behind him. A mountain of parts bobbed across the grass and then spilled onto the ground in a symphony of chaotic crashes.

Standing behind the pile of metal, a young woman stretched out her arms. Thick overalls covered a lady's blouse. Rolled-up sleeves revealed grease smudges along her arms. Her ponytail bounced as she stood straight, and Hobson saw a black streak across her forehead. A ferret in her front pocket poked out his head, as she waved.

Hobson waved back and wrung his cap through his hands. "Hi, Mac. Hey, there little Sprocket."

The professor stepped out and looked over the pile. "Did you get the canisters I asked for?"

She nodded. "I did and I was able to get the last bits of aluminum from this guy I know."

The professor lit up. "That will save so much weight. Excellent work Hazel."

She stuck out her thumb, and Sprocket dove back into the pocket. "I'll get to work on the craft."

The professor mumbled something as he grabbed a canister and rushed off to his workshop. Hobson remained and asked, "Can I help?"

"Sure, bring those big pieces." She grabbed up some netting that held several large chunks of metal and headed off to the silo.

Hobson tried to pick up the same amount she had

and struggled to get a good grip. He adjusted his hands, and when that didn't work, he tried to come at the pieces from another angle. Hobson finally dragged them across the grass, leaving a pair of dug-out tracks. Dropping the piece outside the silo, he brushed off his hands.

"That will do for now," Mac said as she set her scrap pile down. "This place is perfect, isn't it?"

"Professor bought the farm years ago. Far enough outside the city that people don't bother him, but close enough to get supplies. Plenty of space to work."

"No, I meant the silo." Mac opened a door she'd made in the side. "It's the perfect place to work."

"Oh, yeah. It's…perfect." Hobson stepped inside. Before him stood a rocket, bigger than anything he'd seen before. The tall cylindrical craft stood on four fins, each with a rocket attacked. A cluster of rockets were bound together at the bottom of the rocket. Rivets rose up each side in twin rows that showed off the sleek lines. Toward the top, sat three portholes, borrowed from a ship, and the hatch of a submarine. "Wow, looks great."

"I know." She raised her hand toward the rocketship. "Only a few last details, and a repair to one of the backside panels."

Professor Teague's voice echoed from his workshop. "Master Manning…"

"I have to get back. See you, McLachlan." Hobson ran off, leaving her to deal with the rocketship. He hurried into the workshop and found the professor packing the canister with propellant. "Here I am."

"Good, record this." The professor loaded the black goo into the rocket and said, "Quarter-inch nozzle with fifteen grams of propellant X." He glanced over his shoulder, "I am trying a tighter aperture and a stronger propellant."

Hobson set up the camera, replaced the glass plate, and took a photo of the professor. He jotted the figures down in the notebook and then replaced the lens cap. He turned to the professor who shook out his muscles from holding the canister for so long. "Recorded. I should inform Ms. Rutter and Mac about the test. We don't want them wandering in."

"Yes, yes, very good." Professor Teague carried the canister out as Hobson ran to the house and then the silo.

When he arrived back at the professor's side, the wick had already been set, and he was coaxing a flame from the match. They both ran behind the brick wall as Mac stepped out of the silo. The sparks raced into the nozzle and the canister shot into the sky. Flames and smoke roared out the bottom. The professor stepped out to watch his creation soar as Hobson danced with jubilation.

The rocket left a thin ribbon of smoke as it rose out of sight.

"That's the one," the professor turned to Mac. "Bring all the canisters."

Hobson ran over and helped Mac carry the rockets from the silo to the workshop, but after they delivered them, the professor halted all work for the night. The three headed into the house and sat in the conservatory. A knock at the door caused Ms. Rutter to briskly walk down the hall. Hobson turned to the other two. "Who could be here at this hour?"

They heard the deep voice of a man greet Ms. Rutter. A moment later she and a middle-aged man in a dark overcoat stepped into the conservatory. The professor stood up with a smile. The man extended his hand, the professor grasped it, but then pulled him in for a hug.

"How are you, Ambrose?" The visitor asked. "I hope the hour is not too late."

"Not at all," Professor Teague patted the man's shoulder. "We just finished for the day."

"Excellent, I've come to speak with you and check on your progress."

The professor turned to the others in the room, "Forgive my rudeness. Introductions." He motioned to Hobson. "My secretary and dreamer, Hobson Manning." Pivoting to Mac, he held out his hand, "And this is my Engineer, Hazel McLachlan. Allow me to introduce Mr. Ansel Howe, a fellow Vernian and one of the backers of our project."

Mac bristled at the sound of her full name, but still reached out with her thick work glove and shook the man's white-gloved hand. Mr. Howe stared at his palm and then at Mac. Hobson stepped up and shook the man's hand as well. It appeared to shake Mr. Howe back into himself.

"Hello… to you all." Mr. Howe pulled off his top hat and held it to his chest. "A pleasure to be on this grand endeavor together. It was I who said the giant cannon would never work and Ambrose who suggest the Chinese rocket." He spun on his heel and faced Professor Teague. "I must speak with you though, there's been a development."

"Of course, please have a seat." The professor motioned over his shoulder as he led the man to a chair. "Both of you, find something to do with yourselves."

Mac stepped out of the room, but Hobson went to the table with the equipment and pretended to work by picking up and tinkering with some of the gadgets.

"The launch can't wait." Mr. Howe dropped onto a small chair and smoothed out his coat. "You must leave at once."

"Ansel, what are you going about?" The professor grumbled. "We need weeks of tests."

"You don't have weeks." He leaned in closer. "They failed to get the courts or the mayor to stop you, so they're coming themselves."

The professor turned a brass knob on the side of a wooden box on the end table between them, a crystal of rock candy rolled out and he popped it in his mouth. "Who's coming?"

"The zealots."

"Not them again." Professor Teague crunched the candy and smoothed his moustache between his fingers. "This is a scientific expedition." After twisting the end to a point, he waved his finger. "I'd thought we'd explained that we weren't trying to reach God."

"Boyd Miller's followers have been keeping an eye on you. They know you're close. I've heard through an acquaintance that they mean you harm."

The professor popped a second bite of rock candy. "Hardly seems like the actions of good-godly men."

"They've lost reason in their fanaticism." Mr. Howe said shaking his head.

The professor sprang to his feet. "They can't I'm not ready. Nor is the rocket."

A copper canister slipped through Hobson's fingers and clattered on the floor. With a clenched fist he kicked himself, he'd been so silent they hadn't noticed him. He dropped down, snatched it up, and as he stood both men stared at him. Hobson waved.

Sprocket let out a cute little screech. Mac and the ferret popped up behind the two men. "We're actually in better shape than you think. I'm done. I've been making improvements while you solved that whole rocket issue."

Hobson nodded. "We could be ready in hours."

"I suppose fortune favors the bold!" The professor nodded. "Well, you obviously both heard Mr. Howe. We're leaving tonight… or fighting off a horde at dawn." He turned to Mr. Howe. "You know they're coming at dawn. That lot always rises before the rooster."

Mr. Howe nodded and Hobson stood by Mac. The professor pointed to the parts on the table. "Mac, start attaching the rockets. I will get our fuel ready."

"What should I do?" Hobson asked.

"Lock the house down and let Ms. Rutter know we'll be having company."

Hobson nodded.

The professor turned to Mr. Howe. "Care to get your hands dirty in this endeavor?"

"I do not." The gentleman stood and bowed. "Goodnight and Godspeed, Ambrose."

"Thank you."

Hobson began locking the windows on the ground floor as the professor escorted Mr. Howe out to the porch. Hobson ran upstairs and locked those windows too. He even locked the doors so if they did get in, they'd have to get through each one. When he made it back downstairs, Hobson soon found himself in a mad rush, running between Mac and the professor.

First, he aligned all the rockets in a row to make it easier for the professor to load the fuel. Mac, on the other hand, dangled from a rope on her belt attached to a pulley system on the ceiling in the silo. She hung over the side of the rocketship, maneuvering all around, and hammering away on all the parts she'd acquired. Hobson created brackets and struts then sent more rivets, nails, and screws up to her.

Hobson rushed back to the professor as he sealed the nozzle onto a canister. Hobson got the next one set onto the wooden stand, ready for Professor Teague to load. Sitting over in the corner the young man noticed four large canisters against the wall.

"What about those?" Hobson asked.

"They get the second stage up into orbit. Prepare them too."

Hobson stacked each one beside the smaller ones, but a scream echoed from the silo, and both men turned. A cry of frustration. Hobson bolted out the workshop and across the yard. He rushed into the silo and found Mac dangling upside down with a broken fragment of metal in each hand. "The port TransHyperInducer Charging Coil snapped in half. I checked yesterday, and it was fine."

"How bad is it?' Hobson asked.

"We're not going to space without one."

"What do we do?" Hobson scratched his head.

Mac released the belay on her rope and slid down the side of the rocketship. Catching her boot on the rim of one section, she pushed off, flipped, sped down, and landed beside Hobson. "I'll make another."

"Can you do that?"

Mac held up the two parts. "I'll know after I try."

"I'll let the professor know." Hobson bolted out of the silo and ran to the workshop. "Professor." He stopped at the end of the table now lined with rockets. "We have a problem, the port… Trans…Inducer… Coil… is broken."

"The TransHyperInducer Charging Coil—"

"Is broken."

"Broken?" The professor paused and twirled his mustache. His arms slammed down at his side. "We're done. That's it. I can't buy a replacement tonight. It would be weeks before a new one could be sent."

Hobson lit up. "No fears. Mac is making another."

"Can she do that?"

Hobson nodded. "I think she can."

They worked late into the night, pushed on by the tick and tock of Mac's hammer strikes. Hobson tired but found too much to do. Sleep would have to wait until they returned.

As dew settled on every surface outside, and the sky began to brighten, the last canisters were mounted onto the rocketship. Hobson loaded the last skin of water and the final wooden chest of supplies into the crew cabin. He leaned out the hatch. "All ready, Professor." Looking over the house toward town, he saw a line of people with torches. "Trouble's coming!"

Hobson watched as Ms. Rutter appeared from the main house. She hurried to the silo. She didn't head toward Mac, but toward the back, behind the rocketship. He wondered what she could be doing and stepped to the other side.

Opening the porthole, he looked down and saw Ms. Rutter fiddling with the hoses connected to the main rockets. "Why is she here at all?" Hobson wondered aloud, and then he remembered what Mac said about the TransHyperInducer Charging Coil. It had been broken inside its housing, nothing could have struck the coil.

Hobson didn't want to believe Ms. Rutter would hurt the professor's work. Then a flash of light caught his eye from a knife in her hand, and all doubt faded. He spun around looking for something to drop on her, but all he could manage was an exasperated, "Stop! Ms. Rutter don't do it."

Mac popped up from behind a fin and threw her wrench. The tool tumbled end over end and smacked into the back of Ms. Rutter's head. Ms. Rutter collapsed like a sandbag and her blade slid across the floor.

"Why did I just knockout that poor old lady?" Mac glanced up and Sprocket, her ferret, poked his head out of her pocket.

Hobson pointed. "She was trying to cut the hose."

Mac inspected the tubes and connections, running her hand over every surface and putting her ear to the material. When Ms. Rutter stirred, Mac jumped and stepped back, snatching up her wrench. Hobson sprang out the hatch and scurried down the ladder. He grabbed some rope coiled by the door and wrapped it around Ms. Rutter.

Mac waved her wrench. "Make it tight."

Professor Teague stepped in carrying his bags and froze. Dropping his bags, he crossed his arms. "What is this silliness? This is no time for games."

Hobson pointed. "She sabotaged the rocketship."

Mac raised her hand. "I bopped her on the head… that was me."

The professor's face squinches, and with pain trembling in his voice, he said, "Why Hortense… why?"

"You offend God, Professor Teague." She looked at all three of them and her face curled up in disgust. "It's unnatural."

"It is science!" The professor stepped forward, his face blazed red. "I had no idea you were a zealot."

Ms. Rutter turned away.

"Madam, I do not go to offend anyone but to expand human knowledge. We've already taken to the air; it is only natural we push on to the stars."

Ms. Rutter spits her words like a choking engine. "And when you poke the side of the almighty, what do you think he will do? Rain fire or drown us in floods."

Hobson had never thought of God as sitting right above him. The universe was probably huge. The papers had teased the professor, saying he would poke a hole in the sky, or jumble up the stars in his wake. Hobson didn't believe any of that, but he hadn't thought about offending God. How could he offend, when they were pushing the limits of what humans could do?

The professor picked up his bags. "Madam, we are taking a daylong excursion to the stars. Three days at the maximum. I assure you no one, not even god, will be there."

"T'was my job to keep you on the ground and let them know when you were close." Ms. Rutter tried to sit with a proud, tilted, chin, but darting eyes betrayed her nerves.

Hobson had forgotten about the horde. Grabbing his hair, he shouted, "They're coming, or they were coming. They're here!"

Everyone turned toward the house as voices cried out, "Seek thee not, the wrath of the Lord."

"Take her to the house." Professor Teague said pointing at Ms. Rutter.

She yelled at him as Hobson walked her back to the house. He didn't listen to her. He didn't understand why anyone wouldn't want to go into space. Hobson believed that the human race would one day live among the stars. People inhabited every part of the land, soon they would live among the clouds – he'd seen the French designs. If aircities, why not spacecities? Lunar colonies, or maybe settle the abandoned canals on Mars.

Hobson ordered Ms. Rutter into one of the chairs in the professor's workshop. People banged the front door. The walls swayed, and Hobson knew he had to get to the silo. He shut the interior doors on the ground floor and locked them as he had done upstairs. Then ran back to the spaceship.

Hobson climbed up the ladder and into the cabin. Three lush velvet-covered chairs sat bolted to the deck against the outer curved hull. He sat in one, and said, "They're here."

"We're almost out of here." The professor fiddled with the dials, switches, and levers that filled the center console. A globe sat on top of the circular oak console ringed with a ledge of marble veneer. "Focus on your pre-flight checklist."

Hobson nodded and grabbed the clipboard on the side of his chair. He read over the list…

Seal hatches – he walked over and shut the main hatch. Then climbed up a ladder to the observation deck where he secured three more. He locked the handles in place and ran his hand over the glass looking for chips.

Turn on oxygen – Hobson spun the handles on the valve of the oxygen tanks. The hiss of air bulged the tubes that ran throughout the room.

Carbon Dioxide Canisters – Hobson tapped the copper box and slid a lever opening all the vents. The potassium hydroxide inside would capture every exhale.

Secure supplies – He made sure everything was tied down. A web of cords and knots kept the bookshelves and stacks of chests secured.

Check internal pressure – (*gauge must be above the red line and within the green zone.*) Hobson turned to the central console. Most of the dials pointed toward the professor's chair but the one labeled *Internal Pressure* was aimed at Mac's. The dial's hand bobbed above the red line, toward the high end of the green zone.

The last line of the checklist Hobson had added. **Touch the stars**. He circled it and tapped the page with his pencil. Time to soar. Hobson dropped into his chair and said, "All items checked, professor."

Mac popped out from behind the center console. She set her clipboard down and leaned on her big wrench. "All set. She's ready to fly." Sprocket poked his head out of her pocket and nuzzled under her chin.

The professor made some last-minute adjustments to the lever controlling the fins and then reached out for the big leather-clad button.

The silo echoed as zealot's fists tried to replace biblical horns. The pounding shook the tower, which creaked and groaned like thunder in a storm. Hobson froze and clenched up, praying that the structure would hold a moment longer.

"To the stars!" The professor smacked the button and the rocketship lurched.

Explosions rumbled beneath, and the rocketship shot off like a bullet. Instantly, Hobson found himself pinned against his chair as if a giant had sat upon him. His muscles strained as he tried to lift his arms, and he struggled to keep his head facing forward.

The rocketship soared until the deafening roar stopped. The giant disappeared. They paused in mid-air and Hobson was weightless, his arms rose, and he bounced up out of his seat. The professor reached forward and yanked a green-handled lever toward him.

The rocketship started to fall but lurched, and then the professor smacked the leather-clad button again.

The second stage rocket canisters fired, and the craft vaulted higher into the sky. Hobson slammed back into his chair, once again the elephant called gravity sat upon him. The rocketship roared higher for several minutes, and then silence. Hobson could move again. The professor sat up and pulled a second lever. The rocketship lurched as the clamps released and the second stage fell away.

Hobson slipped out of Earth's grip as gravity, a force he'd never not known, disappeared, or weakened so much it no longer affected him. He lifted off his chair and flailed as he swam toward the hatch. He grabbed hold of a pipe next to the door and pulled himself up to look out the window. "Professor, it's astounding!" Hobson motioned, causing him to spin upside down. "The Earth, I see the Earth!"

"In time." The professor started checking the dials. "I need to verify we're going to survive up here. Then ensure we will make it back."

Mac pulled herself along the wall to the door. She gasped and her ferret poked his head out of the front pocket of her overalls. "Professor, you're going to want to see this. This is why we came." Sprocket popped out and spun in a circle until she pulled him close.

Shaking his head, the professor pushed off his chair and slowly floated toward the door. "Oh my, this is delightful." Arriving at the window, he peered outside and his hand snapped to his mouth. "Stupendous."

For the longest moment, the three stared out the windows. The Earth spun below, and the spaceship slowly rolled as they all, planet, craft, and humans danced together through the universe.

The professor pushed off and got to work checking every system. Hobson had a checklist for when they arrived in space. He pushed off and flew down to his chair. "Getting around is the best, who knew gravity was so limited."

The professor tapped a gauge and said, "Yes, I find it most distracting."

Mac laughed and spun around in the air with Sprocket. "So much fun, but nothing beats that view."

After checking off his list, Hobson grabbed his camera. "Quick photograph." He tried to set it up but the camera refused to stay still. It drifted as he did and with the slightest touch would spin or move. He also couldn't get the flash powder to stay in the tray. Locking his feet in the bolted chair, he aimed the camera at the professor behind the console and opened the lens. Counting the minutes in his head, he finally replaced the lens cap and let the camera float in space.

Next, he tried to take one of Earth. The planet rotated too quickly and would never turn out, but he had to try and capture this vista.

Hobson and the professor ran a couple of experiments, testing gravity with different weights—none of which fell. They sighted the stars with a sextant and shook test tubes of oil and water to make sure the rest of Earth's natural laws still applied. Hobson's favorite experiment came when he took a drink of water. At first, nothing came out of the waterskin, then perfect spheres of water floated around him. "Professor."

Professor Teague drifted toward one. "Fascinating. Without gravity, there is nothing to pull the droplet down."

Sprocket tumbled into the droplets and lapped one up with his tongue.

Hobson followed the ferret, floating around with an open mouth. They tasted fine; space hadn't changed the water.

"I thought the stars would be bigger," Mac said pointing out the window.

"I imagine we are still an impossible distance from the stars." The professor said.

Hobson wiped his chin. "I suppose we've proved the stars are more than pinholes in the curtain of night."

The professor nodded.

Mac tapped the glass. "Professor, the planet is being eaten by darkness." Mac pushed back from the porthole. "Oh my, that is night. But how? Nighttime is hours away."

The professor drifted toward the window. "We're headed east, so our days and nights will be much faster."

"Wait. Are we aging faster?" Hobson spun around, but couldn't stop, and kept turning as he passed the others. "Is time moving differently?"

"We won't know until we check the chronometer back at my workshop." The professor sounded giddy until he paused and rubbed his chin. "Well, any clock will do, but we should also keep track of how many days we experience up here."

The spaceship slipped into the darkness and frost formed at the edges of the windows. The professor turned the knob on the wall sconces, brightening the room. They rested as if it were a typical spring evening. Mac and Sprocket bobbed through the cabin, while professor Teague continued to record his data. Hobson tried to settle in his chair but couldn't sit on the cushion. He hovered above it and pulled out an apple to eat.

Reaching into his bag he removed a copy of Jules Verne's From the Earth to the Moon, he figured if he was going to bring one book, it had to be the one that inspired the journey, plus, if they got in trouble it might come in handy.

Taking a bite, he left the apple in the air and turned the page of a book he wasn't even holding. A short time later, as Hobson nibbled on the core, light blazed through the window. Hobson secured the core in a wooden box labeled **bio-material**, pushed off, and peered out the porthole "Professor, Earth is smaller."

The professor rose up and leaned over Hobson. "That's not good. I need to think." He pushed off the wall, spinning as he twisted the ends of his mustache. "If we don't find a way back soon, it may become too difficult."

They were flying away from the planet. Hobson stared out at the stars, which looked no bigger than they did on the ground. A bright orb filled the window, a patchwork of light and dark grey hues. The Moon. Bigger than he'd ever seen it before, it looked stationary just hanging in the darkness. "I had no idea the moon was so far away. I don't think we can reach it."

No one answered him. Both were distracted, figuring out how to angle the spaceship back toward Earth. They were flying away, though. He'd hadn't thought of not returning. He knew there was a chance, but now, drifting away until their air and food ran out... he realized how dangerous this adventure would be. "If we don't get back, at least I got to see the whole Earth first."

As the craft rolled, the moon left the window and another bright orb, this one much bigger and brightly colored with blue, green, and swirls of white. The Earth.

Hobson stared at the blue marble. Everyone and everything he had ever known lay on the small world before him. He looked up and down at the starry sky around the planet. "Wow. Look at it, I can't even see a single city." The globe in the professor's den popped into Hobson's mind. "It looks the same. Professor, North America, looks just as it does on the map… I'm seeing more of the world than I ever could in a lifetime… and it feels small."

The professor looked up from the chalkboard and his calculations. "An astute observation, we will have to make a note. In fact, make a quick sketch."

Hobson pulled out his notebook and tried to capture the moment. He looked down, dissatisfied with his attempt. How could he capture the beauty before him? An odd thought came to him. "All I wanted to do was leave the Earth, and now that I am above her, all I want is to go back."

Mac brushed some loose hairs from her face with the back of her leather glove. "Good one, Hobs." She pulled on her wrench, and said, "You should write that down too."

He pretended not to pay attention, but as he scribbled the words down, he heard her laughter behind him. He sighed, blowing out his breath, and moved backward. A photographer's flash popped in his mind. Hobson spun around and pushed off, floating toward the center console. "Venting. We vent some gas until we're lined up with Earth, then hit the rockets and fly home."

"An excellent plan. I'm already making the calculations on how much we need to vent, and how many rockets to fire off at a time." The professor wiped away part of the equation with his sleeve and reworked the problem.

Hobson watched him, but then moved to a different window.

The professor, who was upside down and still writing, snapped up or down. Hobson would have to figure out how to describe this for his journal. The professor flailed, but then realizing he was upside down, he stopped caring and pointed to the chalkboard in his hand. "I've got it. Hazel, turn the handle on the oxygen tanks. Hobson, when the dial hits the red line, tell her to shut it off."

Mac pushed off and floated up to the level above them. She grabbed two hoses on the ceiling and pulled herself to the handle.

The professor twisted two knobs and flipped a switch. He nodded and Mac turned the handle opening the valve. Hobson heard a hiss and the spaceship rotation slowed.

The needle on the dial dropped, falling ever closer to the red line. As it neared the mark, Hobson glanced out the window, the earth, home, wasn't there anymore. He hoped that meant they were aimed at the planet. He turned back, as the needle reached the line. "Shut it off, Mac."

She spun the handle and the hissing stopped. The spaceship was still, not rotating or rolling. The professor pushed a lever and a popping sound echoed below us. The professor took a deep breath as Mac pushed off and floated down to her seat. Hobson pulled himself over to the window and pressed his face against the glass to look forward. The deepest chill shot through his cheek right to his core and a shiver rippled through him. As he pulled away, he did glimpse the blue marble in front of them. "OH! It's so cold out there. But the Earth is ahead of us."

Hobson pushed off but his back hit the chair. Mac snatched Sprocket out of the air and stuffed him in her front pocket.

The professor slapped the leather button. The rockets fired and they zoomed off.

Hobson pressed against the seat; his legs pressed against the wall above him.

The professor strained his arms to stay at the controls. "Good… another few moments… the rockets will be spent."

Hobson tried to sit up but couldn't move. Contorted, he fought to keep from crumpling. The rockets shut off and the rumbling spaceship settled into silence once again. Gravity returned to zero and Hobson floated off his chair. Shoving off he stopped at the window. "Earth is much larger."

"That's a start." The professor leaned into the center console and tapped on a dial. "We still have to land."

Mac raised her finger, "We should have dinner or lunch… whatever the next meal is. I'm hungry." Releasing the latch, she reached into the basket lashed to the wall beside her and retrieved a round of bread. She tore off a piece.

Hobson nodded and pulled himself over to the basket. He took a sandwich out and set it in the air next to him. The bread slowly parted from the turkey as he went back for an apple. He reached back to take a bite, but the professor threw up his hands. Hobson stopped -mid-bite and Mac's jaw froze.

"Ms. Rutter made that food." He pointed to the basket. "She might have poisoned it."

Hobson pulled away from the sandwich, and it once again began to separate. He stared at the apple, and said, "She didn't make this." He bit in and a loud crunch snapped through the spaceship.

Mac slowly chewed and then swallowed the bread.

She sniffed and touched it with her tongue. Sprocket poked his head out and snatched a bite from the bottom of the bread. If he'd eat it Hobson thought it must be okay. Mac shrugged her shoulders and ate the rest of the bread.

The Earth grew to dominate the windows. Different shades of light brown shifted to deep green on the continents and surrounding them all was the most beautiful azure blue. Swirls of wispy white clouds encircled the sphere, Hobson wished he was an artist who could capture this moment. The photos he'd taken wouldn't do this sight the justice it deserved. "How much would change if everyone could get this view?"

The professor and Mac joined Hobson at the window. A silence settled over the three of them, leaving only a small hiss of air, the tick and tock of a couple of dials, and the rattle of a loose screw.

Hobson smiled. "I don't think I've seen anything more beautiful."

"It is so peaceful." The professor said. "I can't see a single war."

Mac nodded. "But where is that screw?"

As Mac floated along cupping her ear, the professor turned to Hobson. "Let's go home."

Hobson nodded. "How do we miss the oceans?"

"Precise calculations." The professor chuckled and raised his chalkboard. He scratched out a few problems and drew a circle with a line arching into it." He twisted his moustache leaving it covered in white powder, but he smiled and filled the rest of the pad. "I've got it. Get ready to return to Earth."

Hobson pulled himself down to his chair. "Let us return."

They all held themselves down, locking their feet

around the legs. Mac grabbed a leather strap and tied herself to the chair.

The professor noted the compass and double-checked two dials. "One last rocket." He flipped a switch on the center console. Extending his hand over the leather button he paused. "We've gone on an expedition to space, something no one else in the history of mankind has accomplished. We should be proud. Unfortunately, we cannot stay. With this last rocket, we return to our Mother Earth. Back home." The professor checked his pocket watch then pressed the button. "If my calculations were correct, we'll end up back in New York."

Hobson held onto the chair's arms. He wanted to stay but returning alive was more important. Holding tight he closed his eyes.

A soft roar reverberated through the spaceship as the rocket fired. They sped toward the planet. The spaceship shuttered and shook. An orange glow filled the windows. Hobson wiped his brow as the heat inside increased.

"Professor," Hobson said. "Are we on fire?"

"We do seem to be encountering some friction as we re-enter the atmosphere."

"She'll hold," Mac said through gritted teeth. "With the insulation behind the metal and the coatings over each piece, you don't have to worry about her."

The rattling grew worse. Mac stared at the walls, while Hobson lashed himself to the chair. The professor reached out and grabbed a lever on the wall. He waited until the orange glow outside shifted to bright blue. "Ten… nine… eight…" When he reached three, he pulled with all his might and yanked the lever down. Above them, popping sounds were followed by the rocketship lurching. Hobson tumbled forward but the lash caught him, and he held on to the chair. The craft flipped and suddenly the nose was pointed back toward space. They gently swung back and forth, drifting on the wind.

"The dragschutes worked!" The professor pumped his fist.

"Let's hope so." The color drained from Hobson's fingers as he tried to break his death grip on the chair.

The professor scanned the dials and said, "Check the window to see where we're coming down. I may be able to make some adjustments if we're going to hit a building."

Hobson pulled himself into the chair and huffed. Mac jumped out of the chair. She expected to float but fell to the floor. Rubbing her side, she stood up and climbed the ladder to the window. "We're over a city."

"Which one."

Mac pressed against the glass. "Manhattan. I see Brooklyn."

Hobson eased his tense muscles but didn't let go.

"We're really moving…" Mac said while watching the ground. A loud snap echoed through the spaceship and they lurched to the side. Mac fell off the ladder and crashed onto the large cushion on her chair. "I liked floating." She groaned.

"One of the dragschutes malfunctioned." The professor reached out and flipped a switch. Two more snaps reverberated the spaceship and he yanked on a lever. A series of popping sounds above them was followed by a moment of silence, then the spaceship jerked, forcing them all to hold on. "The parachutes will slow us down the rest of the way."

Once the spaceship had settled into a gentle swaying motion. Hobson walked over and stared out the portal on the hatch. "We're getting closer. I see Central Park. I think that's where we're going to land."

The professor smiled.

"I see a parade." Hobson spun around with a puzzled look on his face and then turned back. "Marching band and all."

"Really?" Mac said as she sat up and swung her legs off the chair.

The professor adjusted the trim wheel to angle the fins a bit more. "Mr. Howe might have gone overboard with our arrival… or we're about to ruin somebody's parade."

"The people on the ground are pointing," Hobson said returning the gesture.

Mac scrambled back up the ladder to the window. "Look at all those ladies getting everyone out of the way while those guys just stand there." She laughed. "We're coming down."

"Two-hundred feet or so," Hobson said.

"Brace for impact." The professor said. "Anything might happen"

Hobson rushed over to his chair, as Mac slid down the ladder's rails and bounced into her seat. The professor counted down the distance. Then they stopped so abruptly that the whole rocket shuddered. Hobson looked around and shrugged. "That wasn't so bad."

A loud snap preceded a wobble in the spaceship. It creaked so loud that he thought a woman was screaming. Hobson grabbed the arms of his chair, as the spaceship toppled to one side. Mac fell forward as the professor tumbled up the wall. Hobson remained in his chair, unable to release his death grip or risk falling himself. Once the spaceship settled, he let go and rolled out of the chair.

They hear the muffled murmur of people gathering outside. Mac popped open the hatch and the crowd gasped as she poked her head out.

Hobson followed her, out the hatch. Mac walked along the fall rocketship, and when the professor poked his head out someone yelled, "Are you from Mars?"

Mac fired back, "No, Brooklyn."

Signs for the mayor's reelection dotted the parade. Hobson used a bent fin to slide down to the ground. The professor followed. The mayor stepped out of the crowd and locked arms with Ambrose. The marching bands, jugglers, and firebreathers began to circle the spaceship. The mayor leaned over and asked, "Where did you come from?"

The professor smiled, grabbing the lapel of his off-white suit. "We launched from Long Island. Touching the stars and driving humanity into the next century."

"Local boys, great!" The mayor's smile grew and he pivoted back to the crowd, in a booming voice he said, "Hometown heroes returned from a great voyage to the stars. The world welcomes you back." He leaned back on his heels and shook hands with the professor.

A group of stern faces showed up and stared from the shadows at the back of the cheering crowd.

The professor raised the mayor's hand high into the air. "And we'll be going back soon! One day we will all travel to the stars!" The crowd cheered.

Hobson looked up. He couldn't see the moon but he knew where it was. Turning he looked that way, through the Earth. He wanted to get back into space.

Make a bigger rocket, with cabins and crew. He'd make the Moon soon enough… by expedition.

The End

Doomed Flight
of the
Majestic
Brad R. Cook

Doomed Flight
of the
Majestic

Sometimes bad luck can be the best luck of all.

Rex Fielder stood at the bottom of the stairs, flipping his last quarter into the air and snatching it before it descended. He looked upon the outer hatch of the Majestic, the first luxury airliner, about to depart on its maiden voyage. The immense flying wing would have spanned all of New York's Central Park with two fuselages extending out the back, making the craft look like several planes welded together. He'd never seen anything so massive, so perfectly engineered. Hughes Aviation designed it. No one else could.

Staring at the sleek silver hull, trimmed with blue, Rex thought of how the Majestic would soon be cruising over the white-capped waters of the Atlantic. Reaching down, he gripped the case at his feet and tucked the tripod under his arm. To get this ticket, he'd sold everything he owned, except his suit.

Two women in crisp uniforms greeted him at the top of the stairs and asked for his ticket. He handed over the brightly colored blue paper.

"Welcome aboard the Majestic. Deck one is right down those stairs," the beaming stewardess said.

"Thank you." Rex waved off the porter stepping up to take his bag. Rex didn't have the money to tip him anyway.

The heavy case bounced against his leg as he descended the stairs. The porter passed him carrying two suitcases and a bag. One hit the wall as he went around Rex. A man in a tuxedo, told the porter in a thick accent, "Careful, you…" as a woman in a sequined gown followed. Rex nodded, but they paid him no attention.

Rex found his room, 113, in one of the interior hallways. Most people didn't consider the number thirteen lucky, but when a guy is down on his luck, sometimes bad luck can be the best luck of all.

He opened the door and the reason for a great deal on his ticket came into focus. The room was no bigger than a closet. In fact, most of the broom closets he'd seen looked spacious in comparison. A bed filled one wall, with a small nightstand wedged between it and the other side. Rex slid his case under the bed and leaned the tripod against the foot railing.

"Perfect."

Even this tiny space reflected the vessel's opulence. Gilded French paper covered the walls, and the finest Egyptian linen-draped the bed.

An attendant knocked on the door and stepped inside. He had the body of an athlete, but a face for radio. "Hello sir, my name is Hollis, I'll be seeing to your needs on our journey. Since you are in one of our interior cabins, I'm going to have to ask that you buckle into one of the seats on the Promenade Deck for takeoff."

"Of course," Rex said with a nod. "What about those in cabins?"

"They have chairs and can watch the takeoff from their windows."

"Sounds delightful. Where do I need to go?"

"There is an elevator in the center, or I'd suggest one of the stairwells. There are two forward and two aft." Hollis closed the door.

Rex stepped into a narrow hallway lined with doors. He walked to the stairs he'd come down. All were covered in the same lush burgundy carpet as this hall. With a hop in his step, he jumped up the stairs two or three at a time.

A gold-embossed wooden placard adorned the wall on each floor. Deck five's read Promenade. Rex straightened his tie and adjusted his fedora. The top floor of the airplane had several rows of seats with a wide aisle down the center. A bar sat at the back, and large windows stretched across the front and formed the ceiling above. He walked to the front and stared at the immense runway that narrowed to a point on the horizon. A man in a pinstripe suit, white spats, and an overcoat draping his shoulders walked up beside Rex. Two gentlemen stood two steps behind him on either side.

Rex tipped his hat.

The man returned the gesture. With a thick New York accent, he said, "I'm not staying in my cabin, down below. If this ting crashes… I'll be on top."

Rex nodded. "I couldn't agree more." Then he added, "At least we'd go down in style."

The man nodded, and so did his boys. He pulled out a thick cigar and bit off the end. The gentleman on his left reached out with a gold lighter. "Traveling like kings. Like a boss should."

"They certainly went all out, a real class act," Rex said.

"That they did." The man puffed out a cloud of musky smoke. "And a what exactly do you do, Mr…."

"Oh, Rex Fielder. I direct."

"Really." The man's lip curled, and he took another drag. "Lucius… Lucius Gambino. I've always been fascinated by the… visual arts… if you know what I mean."

Rex swallowed hard. He recognized the name from the papers. He stood beside The Hammer, one of New York's mob bosses. He wanted to ask a thousand questions but worried the wrong one would get him tossed out the window at five thousand feet in the sky.

"Have you made something I might a seen?" Lucius asked.

"Probably not. I'm here to film my first big movie."

"Hey, you must be using, the lovely and curvaceous Veronica Hayworth. I saw her boarding. What a looker."

"She's here, onboard…" Rex wrung his hands together, one of the sexiest screen sirens was on this plane. "I mean, of course, yeah, Veronica is one of my stars. Glad she made it."

"Nice. I remember her in *Gone to Eden*. Whoa." He nudged my shoulder with his thick gold ring. "If ah… you could get me at her table for dinner, I would be most appreciative Mr. Director."

"I'll have to see how she's doing. You know how actors are when preparing for a part."

Lucius laughed, and then his boys joined in. Rex let a nervous chuckle escape the corner of his mouth. He turned as an attendant stepped up and said, "Gentlemen, please take your seats. We'll be lifting off momentarily."

The engines roared to life. Four pairs of propellers spun ever faster until Rex couldn't see the individual blades anymore. Slowly the Majestic rolled down the runway, gaining speed and forcing Rex into his plush seat. As the end of the concrete runway drew nearer, he wondered if the Majestic would be able to get off the ground. Cruise ships didn't fly. Elephants had never soared across the sky. Mountains remained firmly on the ground. But as Rex looked around, the Majestic seemed bigger and heavier than all of those.

As the runway ended, the wheels lifted off, and the Majestic rose into the endless blue above. Rex gripped the armrests as the plane shuddered beneath him. Once they'd leveled off, two women in uniforms appeared and announced, "The captain has obtained a cruising altitude of five thousand feet. He has cleared the amenities of the Majestic to open, and you may freely move about the vessel."

Rex popped out of his seat and rushed back to his room. "Time to get down to work." Pulling the case out, he set it on his bed. Rex opened the latch, and where other passengers carried clothes, his bag held nothing but camera equipment.

Rex checked over the movie camera—the dual-reel magazine, four rotating lenses, and hand-crank—all remained in good working order. He reached in and found only one small canister of film. His uncle let him borrow the camera but only gave him what was in the case. Shutting off the light, the room plunged into darkness. He loaded the film onto the reels atop the camera. There wasn't much, maybe ten minutes worth. He hoped for more, but he wasn't here to make a whole movie. If he could get something great on film, a studio would be certain to give him the money he needed.

With Veronica Hayworth on board, plus New York's wealthiest, he had a chance of getting something worthy on camera.

Hitting the switch, the light came back on, and he was once again able to see. Rex prepped the camera and checked the mounting for the tripod. "Time to find something never before seen on film."

Rex left his cabin and stepped into the lavish dining room filled with white linen tables and fine wooden chairs. He'd left the camera in his room, but it was ready, and so was he. With the who's who on this bird's maiden flight, Rex scanned the room for New York's favorite actors and producers. Before he could find them, a girl in a tight uniform with red ringlets cascading from under her cap stopped in front of him. She had the kind of beauty they made statues out of, but the sweet innocence of having recently escaped a farm upstate.

"Your table is this way, Mr. Fielder." She gestured toward the middle of the room.

Sliding his hands in his pocket, he leaned in and said, "You have a face for movies."

Her jaw tensed as she gestured again. "Thank you. This way."

"I have to call'em like I see 'em." Rex paused a moment longer until she stepped off and guided him to a table near the center. Not on the main isles – where it mattered. "How'd you know it was me."

"I make certain to know the names of all my guests."

Rex nodded. She had a memory like a Dictaphone. The perfect actor. As he reached for the chair, a stiff young man rushed in and pulled it out. Rex sat down, but leaned over and asked, "I didn't get your name?"

The girl shook her head no, and he read it off her name tag – Rita Lake. *Even her name sounded upstate.*

Two tables away, he spotted the famed producer, Mr. Irving Selznick. The corner of Rex's mouth rose. His bad luck was taking a turn.

A couple sat across from Rex. He had a mousey disposition, and she scorned Rex with the same judgmental eyes of a woman who never missed Sunday choir. A red-nosed man beside him sneezed. Pulling a handkerchief from his jacket, the man wiped his nose, which honked as he cleared his sinuses. Rex popped up and said, "Excuse me."

Rex rushed up to Rita. She tapped her fingers over her crossed arms as if she'd been waiting for him to arrive. "I don't have a number, and my measurements are none of your business."

He tried to put on his most charming eyes. "You have to get me away from my table."

"Is there a problem?"

"I think she's going to harm me, and the other guy's allergic to me." Rex caught her glancing toward his table, and then around the room. "Any chance I can get at the third one on the left?"

She eyed him as she bit her lip... then nodded. "Come on, this way. Mr. Costello canceled."

He followed on her heels and bowed to the people seated when they arrived. "Hello."

"Pardon me," Rita said, "Mr. Fielder is in need of a new table, and since Mr. Costello won't be joining us, do you mind if this gentleman does."

Several people motioned Rex to the emptied chair. He slipped in and nodded to Rita who waited a long moment until she stepped off.

Rex delighted in his luck which had spun completely around. He sat with a movie producer, a banker, a former actress, and a couple from Connecticut who had more money than he'd ever see in his lifetime. Plus, Veronica Hayworth was on her way. Rex introduced himself, and made sure to mention that he was from the upper west side… he just didn't mention it was the upper west side of Brooklyn.

The plane shuttered violently, shaking the room, and rattling the tableware. A thunderous crashing sound shattered glasses and people started to scream. Rex grabbed the table as he, and the others stared at the ceiling. Some guests crouched down, some rose to their feet, but the tense glances darting between crewmembers sent Rex's anxiety to the moon.

When the aircraft didn't immediately plunge out of the sky, Rex sighed, lifted his hat, and ran his fingers through his hair. He wondered what happened, but assumed it didn't mean his imminent death. An officer walked into the room and called over some of the crew. Then a passenger in a tuxedo burst in and shouted, "The roof blew off the theater!"

Rex popped out of his chair and ran out of the dining hall. He knew exactly what kind of film would propel him to stardom — a harrowing tale of survival.

Once in his room, he snatched the camera from his bed and tucked the tripod under his arm. Rex bolted back up the stairs. He forced out each breath and labored to take one in as he reached Deck Three. Rex saw signs for two theaters. The Wind and Waves Theater to the right and the Sun Theater on the other side. The roaring whine of the wind echoed from the left.

Rex rushed down the hall. This section didn't sit under the Promenade, but out on the wing. He reached a door and entered the theater. Chairs sloped toward the back of the plane where the stage sat. "Holey Moley!" He leaned back and saw a star-dotted night sky.

Rex glanced over the carnage. Something had ripped through this room. Rex shook his head and set up the tripod. He locked the camera into place on top. Peering through the lens he sighted the torn metal above. The struts reached out into the sky like steel fingers.

He cranked the handle and filmed the damage. Lowering the camera, he captured the crew running around trying to secure the sets and assess the damage. A chair ripped off its broken bolts and flew up out the hole.

"It's so real." Rex paused and rose from behind the camera. "Like no set I've ever seen. I'm a shoo-in for best cinematography."

"You there," one of the crewmen said pointing Rex's direction. "Move along, this area is too dangerous."

"Why aren't we crashing?"

"The Majestic's built to keep flying, even with a few holes."

Rex nodded and waved his hand, but all from behind the camera. He kept the film rolling and captured a large chunk fall from the ceiling. As the flat piece of wood and canvas that used to be the side of a set piece tumbled out into the sky. Rex knew he was getting footage he'd never duplicate in a studio. "I need a story. It can't all be special effects."

Rex shut off the camera and covered the lenses. He rushed back to the dining hall, hoping with each step that Mr. Selznick hadn't left. He sped down the stairs, and rounded the corner, finding several crewmen standing before the doors.

One motioned with his hand. "Sir, I have to ask you to step inside. We're trying to keep the passengers in one place until the situation stabilizes."

Rex nodded. "Excellent… that's why I'm here." It seemed as good an excuse as any to get into the dining hall.

Once inside, Rex found a room in despair. The passengers huddled together, many with their arms wrapped around each other. Terror lay beneath the thin veneer of brave faces. Their eyes trembled, and many remained skittish to every bump of the airplane.

Rex rushed over to the table and froze for a moment upon seeing the silver screen siren Mrs. Veronica Hayworth sitting normally in the very seat he had occupied. Rex bumbled his next steps, and bobbled the camera in his hands, but recovered enough not to crash into the table.

"A camera, really," Veronica rolled her eyes and turned her back. "Irving, what are you trying to pull."

"I swear, I had nothing to do with this."

"Hello again, Mr. Selznick." Rex spiked the folded-up tripod in the carpet and leaned against the camera. "As I said before, I am a director and I know a compelling tale when I see one."

"You can't be serious?" Mr. Selznick sat back and tugged at his bow tie. "Let me guess… our current situation is the perfect movie plot, and you want the money when we get back to recreate all this. Not a bad idea kid, but I'm gonna do the same thing. Only I'll get Fleming to direct."

"Except then it won't have what I have… footage of real tragedy and hero-type action." Rex patted his camera.

"So, you want to cut B-roll for my next blockbuster?"

"No." Rex thought fast, this was his one chance at scoring the deal. "Opportunity and tragedy. Two sides of the same coin. The only question – which one lands face up. I want to cut a film right now. Capture the big scenes of our next blockbuster, and then film the rest in a studio." The slight smile Mr. Selznick kept trying to hide, clued Rex into the first hurdle he'd crossed. Without skipping a beat, he held up his hand, and continued. "I see a love story set on the doomed flight of the first luxury airliner." Rex lowered his voice, he didn't want to cause a panic. "I see a young woman, a passenger… falling in love with, a crewman. The tragedy of the moment drives them together, but her fabulous mother doesn't approve. The villain of the story. See the plane is a backdrop for the real drama."

Mr. Selznick hadn't said anything yet. Rex thought that might be a good sign, and went in for the kill. "Let me burn a dime of celluloid and you won't be sorry."

"I like the pitch kid. But stars, we need stars. And more than ten minutes. Are you planning on asking Ms. Hayworth here if she wants to play another damsel?"

"I'm through with those shrieking damsels. If I play another princess I'm going to toss you off this plane." Veronica flipped her hair, and Rex melted. He'd just been smacked by the silken locks of America's favorite drama queen.

Rex popped back on his heels and snagged his lapel with one hand. The other held up the camera. "Nope. I think the amazing, talented beauty, Ms. Hayworth is going to be the best villain in movies next year." Thinking fast, he turned to her and held out his hand. "Of course, you'd be redeemed in the end. A bad guy turned good kind of way." Both Irving and Veronica turned to Rex, and he knew they were hooked.

Mr. Selznick leaned forward, "My god Veronica that could be a game-changer."

"I like this kid, Irving." She slipped Rex a side-eyed glance that came with the hint of a smile. "He's on to something, me, being bad…"

"I need more." The producer sat back. "What about these lovebirds? How are you going to film this?"

"I can tell you right now," Veronica said. "I am not standing outside so you can get my hair whipping around with the airplane behind me. Give those shots to the lovebirds."

"I… have the other actors already." Rex tried to keep it together long enough to strike a deal. "And I think I can get you the money, but if I do, then I want a producing credit and a real studio contract."

"This kid's an operator," Veronica said, and Rex loved that she used her accent from *Holiday Hi-Jinks*.

"No deal until I see what you can do. But you got your shot, kid. Pull this off, and I can have the contract lined up by the time we land."

"But that's only if we land," The gentleman from Connecticut said. "Veronica do you really want to spend your last moments in front of a camera?"

"I've spent my life in front of a camera, darling. If he is filming our deaths, I can only hope the footage gets released and is a huge hit." Veronica giggled just like in *Gloria*, and Rex almost fell over.

"No, this is an inspirational movie. Upbeat." Rex forced his voice to sound excited. "Let me get the other actors and I'll be back." He headed over to where the crew gathered. Rex spotted Rita toward the edge of the room and tapped her on the shoulder. Rita spun around, and he said, "Can I talk to you?"

She shook her head, and then grabbed an empty tray and headed for the kitchen.

"I want you to be in my movie."

"What?!" Rita spun around and toyed with the small gold cross around her neck.

"Yes, I need you," He dropped to one knee. "You're the only one. Without you, I'm out of luck."

She stopped and eyed him with one brow raised. "Please. You sound like a guy looking for a girlfriend before we crash into the Atlantic."

"Am not." Rex crossed his heart. "A hundred percent telling the truth."

"But now?" Rita set down the tray. "Aren't you worried about the aircraft?"

"Of course, what do you think my movie is about."

"I don't know… I'm not sure I'm ready for a major role…"

"You'll be a natural." Rex jumped up. "I'm offering a once in a lifetime chance. I know you know who I am. I couldn't even tip you, but this is legit. You'd be starring next to Veronica Hayworth, in her next big movie which is guaranteed to take the world by storm."

She eyed Rex with the caution of a girl who heard dreams before, only to see them crash into nightmares. He smiled, used his best I-need-you-eyes, and leaned closer. "You want to be a star, don'tcha? Come on, everybody wants to be a star." Rex pointed his hands at the wall as if framing her name on the marquee. "I can see it, Starring Veronica Hayworth and introducing Rita

Lake."

"My name." She peered over Rex's shoulder looking through his hands. "Let's do it."

He jumped. "Excellent, now you just hang here, I still need to get some of your costars." Grasping her hands in his, Rex beamed so brightly, and she mirrored his exuberance. He brushed her cool, smooth, silken skin with his fingers and the tension in his shoulders eased. Now it was the twinkle in those emerald eyes that pulled him closer. She'd bewitched him, in the best way, but he had to break free. He had a movie to make!

Tearing himself away, he bolted out the door. He waved good-bye as he pushed through the pursers trying to keep the passengers inside. Once free, he ran for his cabin. Skipping down the stairs, he saw his room attendant checking the halls on Deck 1.

"Just the man I'm looking for." Rex rushed up and snatched Hollis' hand before the man had a chance to offer it. He shook with determined force. He'd been taught a strong handshake meant he was serious, and to hold it just long enough to be a little off-putting. "I am in a bit of a pickle, and you, my friend, are the only one who can help."

"How can I be of assistance, Mr. Fielder?"

"Hollis," Rex kept his hand and pulled him closer by his shoulder. "I'm making a movie, and I need a leading man."

"Me?"

"No. The studio would never go for you. They're going to want Cary Gable or Errol Cooper. A name already in lights. But, Hollis, my friend, you could be his body double. When it hits the big screen, take a doll to the theater and say, 'see old Errol Cooper there, I did all the hard parts for him.' Trust me, dames like that kind of thing. And guess what, you'll be bigger than any of them in those pretty little eyes of hers." Rex shook Hollis out of the haze he created. "What do you say? Do you wanna be in pictures?"

"I'll do it for double the daily rate, and twenty dollars up front."

"Twenty dollars! Who walks around with a twenty in their pocket?" Rex let go of his hand. "You're a tough negotiator. Perhaps I'll make you my agent, but come on."

"If I do this, they're going fire me. I need to know I'm covered. This is a good gig."

"I can't deny you that, especially in an age where a fair wage is something the fat cats don't want you to have. All right, I'll see what I can do, but you gotta shake on it. I'll get some greenbacks to wet your whistle, and you act in my movie."

Hollis nodded and extended his hand. They shook more vigorously, and Rex burst away, running up the stairs. He only knew of two people on this plane with money. The couple from Connecticut, but Rex had a feeling they'd be tighter than Fort Knox. They had that *we don't help the little people* type of look. Which only left one man who might give him some dough… to meet the amazing leading lady.

The question, in this moment of chaos and corralling, where might "The Hammer" be hanging out? Only one place came to mind—on top, like a boss! Rex ran up to the Promenade and found Mr. Gambino standing by the windows with his two men. A porter approached, only to be shooed away with a stern gaze from one henchman. A second porter asked them to return to the dining room, but an angry grunt from the other henchman sent the man scurrying off.

Rex took a moment to catch his breath at the top of the stairs. He smoothed out his jacket and said, "Hello again," with a tip of his fedora.

"If it isn't the movie director." Lucius Gambino waved for Rex to approach.

Rex glanced out the window where patchy clouds covered the sky. The wind whined, muffled behind the walls, and he looked up, realizing that only a thin sheet of metal and some luxurious wallpaper kept him from flying out. Gripping the banister, Rex took a deep breath, "I've got a proposition for you, Mr. Gambino."

"Really, and what would that be, Mr. Director?" The man tipped up his hat just enough so their eyes met. "You look like the type of man that needs some dough."

If Rex asked for money, he'd be in the pocket of a gangster. A prospect Rex didn't take a liking to. "You right, I have no dough, but that is not what I need. I'm here for two reasons, because of *your* request, and to ask about these big blokes behind you."

Mr. Gambino leaned forward. "You better start making sense, Mr. Director."

"You asked about Veronica Hayworth earlier. I spoke with her, but first I wanted to ask if one of your boys could star in my movie as one of Ms. Hayworth's..." Rex searched for the right word, one that wouldn't offend either of the large men behind Mr. Gambino.

"Boys," Lucius said.

"Exactly, she needs a... bodyguard. Someone to do things she might not do herself. Anyway, you could meet Ms. Hayworth, and I only need one of them for a few minutes." Rex paused as he saw the reels spinning behind Lucius' eyes. "One last thing, do you have twenty dollars? I have an actor who wants to get paid upfront due to the unique nature of the film."

"I knew there'd be money." He chuckled and his boys joined in. "But I was expecting a lot more zeroes."

"What do you say, are we making a movie?"

"I like ya, so yeah, take one of my boys. Gino has the better-looking mug. He hasn't spent years in the ring at St. Francis' Home for Boys. And here," Lucius reached into his inner jacket pocket and pulled out a billfold. With a flip of his wrist, he opened it and thumbed through several hundreds, fifties, twenties, and fives. He slipped a twenty out and handed it to Rex. "Take this for your temperamental actor, but if he gives you any more lip, you come tell me."

Rex stared at the billfold as Lucius tucked it back into his coat. He'd never seen so much money in one wallet before. "I will." Then Rex realized what kind of talk Lucius would have, and wasn't so certain. "Excellent, thank you, Mr. Gambino. Please join me in the theater in a few minutes. The one that isn't destroyed."

Lucius nodded and Rex ran off. He had much to do and no time to do it in.

Rex rushed into the theater where his actors had gathered. Brimming with eager energy, they turned, already looking for direction. Rex didn't have a clue what to do, what to say, or what he was going to film, but he couldn't let them know. He turned on his most confident smile, and said with an upturn in his voice, "We're making a movie!" Rita lit up, and he delighted in her smile, as well as the one that adorned Hollis and the producer. "Here's the thing, we have a unique opportunity to get some of the greatest footage in cinematic history. I want to shoot the climax now, and then after we get on the ground, we'll film the rest of the movie."

Veronica glided in behind Rex, and in her sultry tone said, "You do know we're going to crash."

"We haven't yet." Rex spun around. "Thank you so much for joining us, Ms. Hayworth. Allow me to introduce the cast. Ms. Rita Lake will be playing the young daughter, who has fallen madly in love over the course of the flight with Hollis, the cabin attendant smitten by her beauty."

"Wait," Mr. Selznick stepped forward and leaned into Rex, "He isn't a box office draw—"

Rex whispered, "He's a stand-in, I'm going to shoot him from behind. We can cast whomever you want later."

The producer clapped his hands and stepped off, "Excellent! We're making a movie!"

Rex motioned for everyone to gather around. The door to the theater swung open and three men stepped inside. "Mr. Gambino, you're just in time. Everyone, Mr. Gambino's assistant is going to play Ms. Hayworth's henchman. He's also helping with the movie."

"My man is here for you." He looked at Ms. Hayworth and slid over like a snake on the hunt. "Well, well, well… Ms. Hayworth, it is my greatest pleasure to be in yer presence."

"A true gentleman, and from New York no less." She shot him a smoldering eye, just like she had in *Sunset Misadventure*. Rex even melted a little, but Lucius' eyes glazed over like prey before the snatch. The snake had met his mongoose. "So, your man is going to be my man… for the picture, of course."

Lucius simply nodded and said, "That's right, like

Mr. Roscoe in *A Hitman for Hire.*"

Ms. Hayworth smiled. "I am so looking forward to being bad."

Rex wavered as she said the line, and kicked himself for not having the camera rolling, but he only had ten minutes, less now. "You're going to be so good at being bad." He gathered the others close around. "The first scene we're going to film is going to be tricky." Rex made certain the camera was secured and popped the tripod against his shoulder.

"Why is that?" Selznick asked.

"Half the actors don't know they're in a movie." Rex walked out the door and the others followed. He went to the damaged theater, where the captain and several members of the crew rushed around securing the aircraft. Rex set up his camera and checked over the lighting as he framed the shot. "You see, I need Ms. Hayworth to demand the captain throw her daughter's lover into the brig, but the captain has no idea, and certainly won't follow a script."

"Easy," Veronica brushed back her hair. "I'll get your shot. It's called improvising for a reason." She stepped off, motioning for Rita to follow. "React to whatever happens and you'll be fine, girly."

Rita rushed after the icon, "My acting coach said I was very spontaneous."

"Come on *spontaneous*, I think I have something that will fit you." Veronica took Rita's arm and they stepped out of the theater.

Rex set up the camera, and turned to Lucius' henchman, "Stand next to Ms. Hayworth and look menacing."

"I can do that."

Rex shot him a thumbs-up, and made a few more adjustments to the camera, changing the lens twice. He couldn't decide if he wanted a wide shot or tight shot. He looked at Hollis, "Stay next to Rita, but don't speak, let them do the arguing. I want you to act with your body, okay."

The crew ran around in the background, getting debris out of the way, and securing the structure as best they could. Ms. Hayworth and Rita entered, both gliding in like gilded statuettes. Rex stopped as Rita approached. Everything melted away, as the crew moved in slow motion. In a short-beaded dress that moved with every bounce in her step, Rita no longer looked like a girl upstate, but the next silver screen siren. Veronica stepped up and pointed to a spot behind her for Gino to stand. Rex placed Rita and Hollis nearby, and angled them toward the camera, making certain his face was turned. The captain kept shooting them odd glances, but he was too busy ordering the crew around to deal with this distraction.

Rex jumped behind the camera and raised his hand. "Action!" Rex paused. He knew he should be cranking the handle, but he had a feeling they'd take a moment to get into the scene and he couldn't waste the celluloid.

Through the lens, he saw Rita's trembling hands clench and release. She eased into the moment and looked to Ms. Hayworth. The seasoned actress winked and then her face hardened, and her eyes turned a dark and steely shade of black. Rex cranked the handle on the camera.

"You!" Ms. Hayworth pointed at Hollis, her voice a mix of power and venom. "My daughter is promised to East Coast American Royalty, not some ne'er-do-well who seduces young girls at dinner!"

The hair on Rex's arm stood on end, as a shudder rippled through him. Veronica Hayworth was going to win an Oscar for this portrayal. He only had to capture her performance.

Rita lashed out and said, "Mother, we love each other."

"How dare you run off with this…bellboy!"

"He's… that isn't even important now. The plane is in danger."

"If we die today, you will not die with him."

"Mother, no!" Rita yelled and clutched onto Hollis.

Veronica stormed over to the captain, "I demand you throw this man overboard!"

He spun around in genuine shock, "Madam, I cannot. I will not throw a man into the sea."

"I demand you keep this boy away from my daughter!"

The captain looked at Veronica and then to the young couple. "I don't have time for this. More important matters demand my attention!" He started to walk off but stopped. "I can order all of you back to the dining room, and you," he pointed at Hollis, "back to your post!"

Hollis nodded, and Veronica threw up her hands, "Henchman, separate them!"

As Gino rushed forward, the crew erupted in chaos. Shouting and pointing caused the captain to run toward the other side of the room. Rex zoomed off of the actors to film the frenzied crew. Through the lens, he saw them surround a small bundle of tubes with red and white wires… a… bomb.

Rex bit his lip to keep from yelling the word. He might be telling the world's greatest disaster story, but the gaping hole in the ceiling wasn't his only problem. A bomb meant this tragedy wasn't an accident, but sabotage. Someone was trying to bring down the plane. He thought about getting the film out of the camera and into containers, but there wasn't time. The captain grabbed the bundle and tossed it out the nearest hatch. An explosion shook the craft, but the minor turbulence passed quickly.

Rex stopped cranking the camera's handle. He wanted to stay on the captain, but he had to get to the next scene. Rex now had another problem. He'd thought this was an accident, but someone was trying to bring down the plane. Maybe he was filming their end? He agreed with Veronica, if this was the end, then he would make certain to leave a stunning legacy.

Finish the film. Get it in the can. Then put the can in something indestructible and wrap it in something that floats. He repeated it a few times in his mind as he worked out the next shot.

"All right, that scene is in the can!" Rex clapped his hands together to draw everyone's attention. "Ms. Hayworth, that was simply stunning. I have chills." He turned to Rita, "You were great. When you screamed out *mother*... so believable."

A coy smile slipped onto Veronica's lips, and Rita lit up.

Rex moved everyone into the main hall, which ran between the two theaters and acted as the central corridor for the craft. He looked for the best angle as crewmen rushed back and forth in a panic.

"For this scene, the chase is on." Rex motioned toward the long corridor. "The lovers are fleeing down the hall, escaping the mother and her henchman. Rita, you and Hollis exit and run to the end of the hall. Gino, you burst through the door, and run after them. Veronica, you come through behind Gino, but stay at the door."

The cinema siren tossed back her long locks, "Exactly. I would not give chase when I have muscle for that."

"You're so in character. Love it."

Mr. Selznick, the producer, stepped up behind Rex as he set the camera and checked his sight lines. "You're onto something. If we survive, let's have lunch at Delmonico's when we get back to New York."

"It's on my calendar." Rex turned back to his actors. As they slipped into the theater, he cried out, "Action!"

Rita threw open the door and rushed into the hall with Hollis. As Rex cranked, he hoped Hollis wouldn't turn toward the camera, and he didn't. The pair stumbled into the center of the hall. As the door swung shut, Gino plowed through, his shoulder lowered like a high school linebacker. Veronica rushed out right on his heels. Pointing she screamed, "Bring her back to me!"

The plane shuddered and listed heavily to one side. Rex struggled to keep the camera steady. Mr. Selznick and Mr. Gambino grabbed the railing on the wall. Gino chased Rita and Hollis down the hall, but the lovers tumbled onto the carpet. They hopped up and rounded a corner.

"Cut! Grab hold, everyone!" Rex scooped up the tripod, clutched the camera close, and slid his arm through the railing on the wall.

Gino fell, sliding along the carpet into the wall. Veronica clutched the door, but it swung open and slammed against the wall. Lucius ran forward to aid her while his other henchman went hand-over-hand down the railing.

The plane leveled off. Rex found his footing and steadied the camera. He looked around for his cast and found them huddled in small groups, but uninjured. Rita and Hollis rushed back. Lucius helped Veronica, and his other henchman lifted Gino to his feet.

Rex put on his best you-got-this smile and said, "Even the transition scenes in this movie will be amazing. Ms. Hayworth, that was stunning, very powerful. Gino, thank you. Great work. You okay?" The large man nodded and Rex pointed, "Nice expression."

Rita stepped up with wide eager eyes. "We thought we'd ruined the take when we fell."

"Not at all." Rex seized her hands with his free one, pulling her closer. "Stupendous. You were great." He turned to the young man, "Hollis… you didn't look at the camera, even after falling. Excellent!"

"What happened to the plane?" Mr. Selznick asked. "Is this the end?"

Rex shrugged. "Not sure, but we seem okay for now."

Rita chimed in and pointed down the hall. "We saw a couple run out of an access door down there."

"Yeah, and it's Employees Only," Hollis said.

"Maybe you should tell the captain, Hollis." Rex didn't want to lose his actor, but he really didn't want to crash. "Make sure you come right back. We're about to film the climax."

He nodded and darted off.

"No rest for the rest of us. We need to get the final shot in the can." Rex, the mad piper with a movie camera, slipped into the damaged theater, and the others followed. Everyone stared at the gaping hole above. Rita pulled closer to Rex. With his trademark I-got-this smile, he said,

"This is where we get the Oscar."

"This is where we all die," Veronica said, with her legendary sass.

Rex set up the tripod and spun around. "This is going to be epic." Hollis ran into the theater, and Rex continued, "Veronica, you've caught up to the lovers. Gino, I want you to have them. Rita, with nowhere else to turn, you're going to accuse your mother of trying to stop you from being with Hollis, by sabotaging the plane. Veronica turns to Gino, it wasn't her, he went too far. Gino, you deny it. Then the plane will shake, we'll all fall to the ground like the plane had lurched again, and finally, mother and daughter will have a big reunion."

"I love it!" Mr. Selznick clapped his hands together.

Rex set up his camera and checked his shot. Wind whipped torn fabric and sent tiny bits of debris everywhere. The wind whined and buffeted every non-rigid surface. He positioned Veronica on the lower level and sent Rita and Hollis to the balcony. Gino followed. They were far enough away from the hole that Rex wasn't worried, but through the lens, it looked like they might fly out at any minute. "All right, give me power, give me drama. Give me your all! Action!"

Veronica reached out. "Seize them."

Gino lifted Hollis by his uniform's collar.

Rita screamed out, "No!" She spun around to face Veronica, pressing herself against the banister. "Mother! Stop this, I love him. Tell your man to let him go."

"I and I alone know what is good for you." Veronica's grand gestures made Rex's knees go weak. "I'll not let you waste our lives. Everything I've done is for you."

Tears flowed from Rita's eyes as she collapsed

against the railing, pleading with every ounce of her soul. In a flash, anger filled her eyes. "Wait, it was you. All of this was caused by you."

"Every action I take is for this family."

"You blew up the Majestic! You're going to kill all these people just to spite my heart."

"I had plans for you, young lady."

"I had plans too!" Rita pushed off the railing and slammed her fists against Gino's chest. He loomed above her, unaffected. She turned back to Veronica, "How could you do this?"

"I told my man to damage some part of the plane so the crew would be too busy to speak with you. He went too far."

Gino yelled out, "I did like you asked, boss." He pointed at the hole. "But I didn't do that."

"Don't you see, mother? We all have to pay for your fear, your loathing, your hatred!"

"I…."

The Majestic lurched and listed to the side, sending Rita tumbling over the railing. She snatched the polished wood, and Hollis rushed forward. Because he had to grab hold of her and the rail, his face remained obscured from view.

Veronica rushed forward despite the slanted floor. "Hold on, don't drop my baby."

Rita screamed, "Mother!" and slipped through Hollis' hands. She fell the last few feet to the carpet below.

Veronica rushed up and clutched her daughter. "I'm sorry. I don't want to lose you." Veronica looked up at Hollis. She didn't say anything, but with the pained expression on her face, everyone would know her heart had turned.

A crewman ran into the frame and pointed toward the far wall. "Stop the saboteurs."

Gino spun around and drew a pistol. Several crewmen ran by Rex, who zoomed in and found the couple he'd seen when he first boarded ducking out of one door and running toward another.

Lucius and his henchman rushed forward with guns drawn. The captain and several crewmen followed. The couple raised their hands when Lucius motioned with his pistol.

The captain forced the couple to turn around and took a pair of handcuffs from his steward. As the iron locked around their wrists, Rex heard the film flapping in the camera. The end. He stood up as the captain shook Lucius' hand for helping capture the real saboteurs.

A month later, Rex arrived at the studio and stepped into the Majestic's theater. The crew had replicated every detail. Mr. Selznick even sprang for the original plans to make the set exact in every way. Instead of one camera, Rex now had three. No longer limited, endless rolls of celluloid surrounded him.

Rita ran up behind Rex and snagged his arm, "Isn't it amazing?"

"It's almost like being back on that flying death trap." Veronica sauntered up in an evening gown made by Coco Chanel. "I'm not sure if we even survived…"

"Or is this all a dream?" Rita kissed Rex's cheek.

"This is the movies. Dreams never die." Rex smiled at his leading lady. His luck had landed sunny-side up.

Next came weeks of filming, months of editing, promoting, the premier, and then the awards. The buzz around the flight already had moviegoers lined up outside the theaters, and with Veronica in the papers every other day alongside Lucius, New York's "*reformed*" number one citizen, the box office would be bigger than *Queen of the Nile*.

Rex flipped a quarter into the air. As he reached out, Rita swooped in and snatched it. His head popped forward as Veronica smacked him with her clutch, "Come on, kid, let's send this plane into the big blue ocean, and all get Oscars."

The End

Brad R. Cook
A Clockwork Heart
Award Winning Steampunk Short Story

A Clockwork Heart

An award-winning short story

Obadiah's heart had cracked, been repaired, and shattered again. Now the pieces lay in the bottom of his chest clinking together whenever he walked.

The depths of this depression hadn't been reached overnight, or even a couple of months. It took years to reach this barren rock bottom. He tried to figure out where it began and even created an intricate chart that spanned three walls of his workshop. Strings wrapped around push pins marked out all the connections of his life. How tragedies had strung themselves together in a linked chain. Small bits of parchment with notes scribbled in ink had been pinned to each point where the strings connected. Circled in white chalk were the biggest tragedies.

What had Obadiah discovered? Tragedy followed him, stalked him his whole life, and new depths came after every plateau. He spent three months tracking his entire life and at the end, standing in the center of his shop, he wished he had never started.

Death was one despair. It started when he lost his parents at a young age and continued into his twenties when his wife and child were swept away by the flu.

But now he had a plan and had spent weeks perfecting it. He just needed his assistant to help.

He watched Lilly through the octagonal window in his workshop as she stepped out of her father's house and began her daily mile-long trek to his clock tower.

Obadiah, the clockmaker, lived atop a small mountain at the edge of town. His tower held a two-story clock face on each of the four sides and was visible from anywhere in the isolated valley.

A wrought-iron circular staircase wound around the tower until it stopped at a door. Lilly's gloved hand slid smoothly along the metal railing which creaked and groaned like a grumbling bear, as it did every morning and evening. The stairs acted like a doorbell, ensuring no one surprised him. Obadiah didn't like surprises.

He heard the heavy bolts slide out of place as the tower door opened. "I have arrived with lunch," she called out and stepped inside.

Obadiah didn't answer, he used to come down from his workshop and they would enjoy lunch together, but over the last week, he had said nothing and remained locked inside.

Through the glass floor panels in the center of his workshop, Obadiah watched as she lifted the hem of her long skirt and climbed the internal wrought-iron stairs.

Lilly knocked on his workshop door. He continued working, she distracted him enough and he needed to focus. The round door rolled open. He turned stunned. In all the time she had worked for him, she'd never entered his shop without asking him first.

"Lilly, what are you doing in here?" He spun around fidgeting with the delicate tool clutched in his hands.

"I wanted to make sure you were okay. I worry when you lock yourself away in the workshop. The last time you devoted yourself to a grand invention, you created the Mayor's new clock, but became sick from not eating."

"I remember that clock, it told not only the seconds, minutes, and hours, but also the day, month, year, even the phases of the moon and the position of constellations. Once an hour, a small door opened and a tiny soldier stepped out to sound a horn."

Her soft smile lit up his dingy workshop. "It is my favorite, and the mayor still cherishes it to this day."

He shuffled off to dodge her compliment. Passing the mirror, he'd set up to bounce light through a prism, he saw an unfamiliar face staring back. Dark circles outlined his soft eyes. His disheveled hair looked as if he'd been running his hands through it over and over, but never once with a comb.

"You're wearing the same white shirt and brown vest I gave you three days ago." She shook her head and held out the wicker basket in her hands. "Come, let's eat some lunch."

"Lunch?"

"You have to eat something; to keep up your strength."

"Lunch?"

Lilly shook her head. "You've been working since I left yesterday, haven't you?"

"What?" Obadiah pulled out his pocket watch and flipped it open in his palm. "Look at that, it is tomorrow."

"What are you working on?"

His gaze lifted from the internal calculation of where the time had gone and he snapped shut his pocket watch. "My greatest masterpiece! Today, I repair my broken heart."

"How?"

He always found it sweet the way she paid attention even when he started to sound unhinged. After several minutes, marked by the tick and tock of the giant clock above, even he was wandering from his description of each individual part. "I'll show you." Obadiah spun around and walked deeper into the workshop.

Lilly followed.

Above, below, and around them, all the intricate gear work, crankshafts, and counterweights moved in syncopated rhythm, kept in time by the pendulum passing back and forth in the center of the room. A melody filled this beautiful chamber rather than the repetitive demands of a ballet teacher's cane. It reminded Obadiah of his first workshop, next to Madam Ludmilla's dance academy. He'd always enjoyed the metronome-like beat.

She stared up at the clockwork above as they crossed the room. "Do you like staring at the gears? Seeing on a massive scale what you work on in miniature."

Obadiah paused and looked around. "I never thought of it like that…but I suppose I do."

On a large workbench, numerous tools sat neatly arranged beside a small fist-size object made of leather, brass, and bronze.

"That's an odd clock." She said as her brow scrunched up. "Is this what you are working on?"

"Yes, and it's almost ready." Obadiah pulled off his glasses which had a series of multicolored and various sized lenses attached by tiny bronze arms that allowed him to see the world in minute detail.

"What is it? It doesn't look like a clock."

"It's a new heart—one that cannot break."

She cocked her head to the side. "Is that even possible?"

"Of course. The heart is a simple pump, pushing both blood and emotion through our veins."

"The heart is far more complicated." A soft smile parted her lips. "Please eat some food. I stopped by the baker this morning."

He flipped open his watch, stared at it for a brief moment, and then tucked it back into his vest pocket. "I need you to contact my friend the barber, he must come today. Tell him to bring his surgical tools."

"Of course, right away." Lilly started to leave but paused. "For a haircut?"

"No, he will understand." Obadiah wanted to spare her the more gruesome details.

She stepped toward the door and wiped a tear from her eye. "I shall return with the barber and a plate of food for you."

He nodded and grumbled under his breath. "Yes, yes, that is fine…I need to adjust the…" Lowering his head, he focused on the intricacies of the clockwork heart. Obadiah popped up. "Use the auto-writing telegraph on my desk."

Lilly rubbed her shoulder as she sat as if relieving an ache within. She composed the message on a piece of parchment. Several brass arms attached to the pen, led to the telegraph machine, where a series of tumblers changed each letter into dots or dashes. The signal zipped along the wires to the person named at the top of the letter. Across town, in the barbershop, she knew the message would be written out by another of his many inventions.

Lilly read the message aloud. "Dear barber. Stop. The clockmaker requests that you bring your surgical tools to his tower. Stop. Thank you, we look forward to seeing you soon. Stop."

Her tears fell upon the parchment, but Obadiah ignored them, he had much to focus on before the surgery.

She slowly slipped off.

The last details consumed him and her absence went unnoticed until he heard her rap lightly upon his workshop door.

"Come in, come in." Obadiah awkwardly turned as his automatic responses failed him. He led Lilly to a table he had set up with glass vials and rubber tubes strung up like decorations on some kind of industrial tree. "I've gotten everything ready, I just need you—"

Lilly stopped and clasped her hands together. "I must speak. I cannot let you do this. I want you to be happy, to love life again, but this operation could kill you. Is death really preferable to a broken heart?"

Her outburst stunned him into silence. He started to explain, but Lilly dropped the basket of food. Her hand seized her chest, her eyes rolled back, and she collapsed on his workshop floor.

"Lilly!"

≋   ≋   ≋

A muffled ticking filled the chamber as Lilly slowly opened her eyes. Light poured in, reflecting off the crankshafts and gears above.

Her fingers drifted to the linen wrapped around her chest. After the first touch, she retracted her hand but slowly slid it over the bandage sticky with blood. "What is this?"

Lilly tried to sit up, but Obadiah gently encouraged her to lie down. He whispered, "Keep still. I don't want you to tear your sutures."

"My what?"

"Sutures." He blotted each drop of sweat from her forehead with a cloth. "I was so worried. Your heart gave out. The barber and I thought we'd lost you."

"My heart? Did I die?"

"For a time, but it's okay, I gave you a new one."

Lilly's eyes went wide. "But that was the cure for your sorrow."

Obadiah took her hand. "When you collapsed—my heart crumbled. I realized I couldn't lose you. I never knew how much I needed you until you were almost gone."

Tears welled in his eyes, through all his sorrow; she had never seen him cry until now.

"But what about your heart?"

"When you drew breath once again, I found my heart not only whole but had grown in size."

Electricity jolted through her as he gently kissed the top of her fingers.

"I cannot live without my Lilly." The sorrow that had weighed Obadiah down, and drained him of life, shattered.

Her fingers intertwined with his. "Will I be okay?"

He nodded. "As long as you wind up your heart once a month."

"Thank you," she said and pressed her lips gently against his rough knuckles. "I don't know what else to say, but thank you."

"Say that you will never stop coming to my workshop."

She wiped the tears from her eyes, bit her lip, and smiled. She nodded.

"Oh, you'll need these." He placed two ornate brass keys on her palm. "To wind your heart."

Lilly placed a key back in his hand. "I want you to keep one."

The End

The Legend of Spring-Heeled Jack

a horror/steampunk short story

Brad R. Cook

THE LEGEND
OF
SPRING-HEELED JACK

English Countryside, 1842

Lucy stepped out of the theater, the viscount's ballroom which he'd had arranged for the production. In step with the joyful tune of the nearby quartet, she glided across the azure rug. In her cornflower gown, she visually fit perfectly into the room and it made her heart rise. Hopefully, she could be so easily a part of the viscount's life. Her fingers, however, refused to stop picking at the button on the wrist of her gloves. The viscount would return momentarily, champagne in hand... like a prince, and she a princess.

A dark cloud approached nicknamed the *Mad Marquess*. He circled like a storm on the horizon, one that threatened to dump rain on her perfect evening. He nudged his mate and she knew, all women knew, the predator was on his way. Lucy turned her back and stiffened, hoping he would go away.

"Lucy... Lucy, how are you on this night? A night ignited by luna's round face." The marquess slid on his polished boot up next to her.

Lucy jumped and clutched her hand close to her

chest. "Marquess, you should carry on, my lord. I've asked you not to—"

"You look lovely tonight, like a statue set against the sky…"

Lucy eyed him. "I am a statue in the sky?"

The marquess wrung his gloves through his hands. "I mean no, of course not, that makes no sense. You look like a statue on the blue…"

Lucy shook her head wondering if she'd hear him right. Though she did enjoy seeing him stammer. "I am a blue statue? I'm afraid I do not understand."

"No, you are art, because of the rug." The marquess thrust his arms out pointing at the floor. "Your eyes bewitch me."

She took a step back, and he moved forward.

A shrill but firm voice behind them says, "Good evening, marquess, what business have you with my Lucy."

As the viscount took her hand, the heat of his fingers released her tension like a knife through corset strings. The marquess turned away but then whipped back.

Through gritted teeth, the marquess said, "Viscount." He reached out to grab Lucy's arm, but she spun to keep his grimy fingers from reaching her.

The viscount, stepped between the marquess as Lucy swept her arm back toward the hall. "Why don't we all return to our seats, the production will resume shortly?"

The marquess' hand balled into a fist. "Why don't you. I must speak with the lady about her intentions."

"I have no intentions with you, sir." Lucy shot him a side glance, burning eyes couldn't hide the rage of his words. "I have told you no in every way granted to us by the English language, and even once in French. I can say it in no other way."

"But I wished to be your escort."

"Never with the *Mad Marquess.*"

The nobleman winced from her words, and Lucy hoped that would be the end of it, but she feared she'd only made him worse. Everyone had murmured for weeks, how he and his boys prowled through the night hunting for maidens. Even if the ladies of court were exaggerating, she had seen the white circles around his iris, his wicked wide-eyed look of terror. The memory of that first no, his reaction unsettled her so badly she couldn't even attend her music lesson. Her joy drained quickly. What would the marquess do next to ruin her perfect evening?

The viscount pulled her off, taking her from this villain. He led her back to her seat by the stage. The house lights dimmed and once again the actors carried her away in a dream. The play, a tale of the Black Dog of Suffolk, frightened and excited her, but she didn't want to miss a minute. As the audience gasped at the appearance of the beast, Lucy leaned forward. As the actor stalked the stage on all fours, he moved so well she started to believe he was the beast. Her hands wrung the folds of her dress, and she jumped as the beast leapt out and attacked the hero.

She turned for reassurance from the viscount, but terror etched itself on his face. She wished him to be a knight, but he looked more like he wanted to run. However, he had protected her from the marquess. She smiled and he returned the gesture. The beast growled and she snapped back to the stage.

At the end, the viscount escorted her out to the main hall, where an attendant waited with her shall and muff. "I wanted to get you out of there to avoid the… the *Mad Marquess.*"

"Thank you." Lucy looked around for the nobleman. "I do not see him."

"He did not return to the theater." The viscount put his hand on her back to guide her toward the carriages. "Allow me to escort you home, for your safety."

Lucy tucked her hand in her muff to warm them. "We have no chaperone."

"My driver will guard your honor. I promise to keep my hands above the carriage blanket."

"I accept." Lucy worried she might need an armed guard to protect her from the marquess, but if nothing else, she would be warm with the viscount close beside her.

The viscount motioned with his hand and a single horse with an open carriage pulled up in front.

Lucy stepped into the carriage and the viscount sat beside her. The driver helped get them under the thick wool blanket. His knees touched hers, and though her heart didn't skip a beat as she had hoped, it was nice to have him as company. His slight warmth did help as well. He shifted beside her, constantly adjusting himself. The driver's sweet smile put her at ease, but the viscount wrung the blanket in his hands.

Lucy smiled. "The play was thrilling."

The viscount snapped her a look and nodded. "Yes, but perhaps a bit too frightening."

"The beast wasn't the only monster there tonight. She nudged him, "Thank you for being my knight tonight."

"It was my privilege, milady."

Lucy laughed. He mocked her status, but in a playful way. "Let us hope we avoid the monsters, I heard about the young girl across the river."

"Tragic. She was slashed. I spoke with the Lord Mayor the other day. He's taken to traveling the roads on some nights."

"Do you think it could be…" Lucy hesitated, her throat sore and scratchy as if she couldn't say its name.

"Spring-Heeled Jack?" The viscount raised his hands as if they were claws and laughed. "No that's just a myth. The legend is older than my grandfather. The girl was attacked by an animal."

"That's a relief." She released her held breath, to let her body relax, but a hoot in the night sends her from her skin. The darkness around her shrouds all manner of creatures. Her eyes saw only dark shapes and shadows shifting all around her but nothing clear, only gifts for her imagination to play with.

Her heart pounded against the whale bones in her corset, the viscount kept turning and smiling to initiate some contact, but her eyes never left the darkness. *He* was out there somewhere.

As they turned down a lane with overgrown trees rising behind stone walls, the viscount wrapped his hand around hers. "You're cold, let me warm you."

They slid closer, and as she smiled.

The horse neighed. The driver tugged the reins. "Calm down their girl." A sound, a metal *schink*, echoed out of the darkness. There is a loud hiss in the night. A pair of thumps shook the ground and her core. The driver, the viscount, and Lucy turned toward the left side of the road. From behind the wall, a man in a cape soared over and slammed down beside the driver, splintering the wooden bench.

The old man yelled out, yanking back on the reins. The horse reared, its cry shattered Lucy and she screamed.

Perched on the carriage, the creature, thrust his arms out, revealing a scalloped black cape, the dark waistcoat underneath had white skeleton ribs painted on. The bright moon reflected an eerie light off the red lenses in the helmet's goggles. Pointy spiked horns protruded from the top of the helmet like ears. Long, shiny, sharp curved talons on the end of each finger pointed at her.

This caped-man threw back his head and filled the night air with a wicked cackle. With his gauntlets splayed wide, he slashed the driver. The old man raised his arm to defend himself, but this creature slashed twice more, leaving deep gashes along the driver's face and forearm.

Crimson drops dripped from the metal tips of the caped-man's gauntlets. Lucy retracted, hitting the seatback behind her. Trapped by the thick blanket and the lacquered carriage, terror ripped through her like wildfire. Beside her, the viscount's wide, panicked eyes engorged this evil, red lenses set in dark bronze loomed over the viscount as if this man fed off their fear. Joy, lust, and rage echoed out of the helmet as he cackled.

Lucy screamed but was drowned out as the viscount shrieked and flailed. His eyes wide in mortal fear. The old man slumped in the driver's seat, dragging the reins with him. The caped-man clicked the heels of its thick metal boots and sprang into the air. The carriage crashed into the ditch, clattering back and forth, as the reins tangled the horse. Lucy held on to the carriage rail.

Landing on the stone wall, the caped-man turned and hissed.

The carriage rested at a slight angle. Beside them,

the figure perched on the wall, his claws scraped against the stone below. He hissed, clicked the heels of his metal boots together, and leapt back onto the bench.

"Spring-Heeled Jack!" The viscount shrieked in a shrill tone. Kicking, the nobleman whipped up the blanket. Metal talons slashed the cloth to tatters.

The caped-man snatched the viscount in his claws, the nobleman fell silent and slumped over. Passed out, his tongue hung from the corner of his mouth like a dog.

"Away demon!" Lucy clutched the small cross around her neck.

The red lenses turned toward her, he opened his clawed gauntlets and the viscount dropped into the seat.

Lucy wedged herself into the corner of the carriage. Her heart punched her ribs. Tears streaked down her cheeks. This caped-man pricked her skin with his metal talons. She squirmed and thrust out her arms and legs. He laughed and hissed, "*Never with the Mad Marquess.*"

She drew in her breath and screamed. This mad monster was the vile marquess.

Laughing wildly, he slashed at the draped cloth of her dress, revealing white knickers underneath.

She screamed, but he neither heard nor cared.

"I'm Spring… Heeled… Jack!" He yelled into the night. He flared out his cape and threw back his head to unleash another devilish cackle. Lucy drew a deep breath as shadows enveloped the moon, plunging the night into ever deeper darkness.

Something darted back and forth, running wildly across the yard. A man's scream drew the marquess's attention back to his carriage. Lucy turned as well, but in the inky darkness, she could only make out shapes, but grunting, tearing, crunching, demonic snarls echoed out of the night. A man screamed.

The marquess whimpered, "Jacob?"

In the darkness, a pair of burning red eyes, like small globes of fire, leered from the distance. Lucy couldn't look away, but all she saw were eyes, not the outline of whatever held them. The shadow pulled away from the Moon, and once again moonlight illuminated the night. A dark figure perched on a man's chest, the body twitched uncontrollably beneath the beast.

The marquess froze. Lucy's chest heaved as her heart pounded inside. She wanted to move, but her body refused her commands.

The red eyes were set deep in sunken sockets. The creature's pointy chin and ears framed a snarl, revealing long white fangs. Skin like charcoal clung to its bones. Drawing its fingers out of Jacob's chest, steel tips embedded in its flesh, glistened with a crimson hue.

Long and lanky, the creature dug its foot into the ground beside Jacob. Running down the back of its legs, jagged flesh wrapped around metal pistons and a large coil spring pressed into the creature's flesh. The skin clung to the metal as if it were bone. Wisps of steam and smoke rose from the mechanics, which glowed with an unholy fire. Horns rose out its head and extended off the elbows and ankles.

The marquess' body twitched as he tried to move, but remained cemented. Lucy didn't think this was another noble, a joke by local boys, or a setup by the viscount. She knew she needed to flee. The voice inside her screamed to leave, but the marquess still pressed against her pinning her down. The marquess's eyes remained fixed on the demon's burning gaze. She willed herself to move. She would not be a moth burned in the flame. She would fight… but as she rose, the creature flung Jacob's body against the wall. The sound of the smack, the crunch of bones, and the undead groan that echoed within the body as it slumped to the ground terrified her to the core.

Above her, the marquess raised his hands and splayed his gauntlets. An unholy, guttural, cackle rumbled out, as the creature threw back its head and laughed, shaking the ground and Lucy's whole body. Even the stones in the wall trembled.

The marquess glanced down at Lucy. She saw terror in the eyes behind the red lenses. His gauntlets rattle against each other as fear shook him.

Wispy clouds of steam enveloped the creature as it sprang off, landing on the narrow wall, its curved metal claws sank into the stone beneath like they were nothing more than loaves of bread. The creature seized the marquess by the shoulder and ripped him from the carriage. Hot breath, harsh with the odor of bile, blasted over marquess and wafted over Lucy. The two were only a few feet from her but sulfur and brimstone assaulted her senses. Flaming red eyes glared at the nobleman. The marquess squirmed but was locked in the creature's clutches.

The horse neighed, and Lucy's voice broke through the night. "By God, what are you?"

Thick boney spikes protruded from the creature's arms as charcoal skin clung to its skeleton. Lucy noticed every rib as the demon lifted the marquess with an otherworldly strength.

"*I am* Spring-Heeled Jack!" A deep guttural voice echoed within this creature.

"Please…" Marquess tried to speak, but the words clung to his throat.

Lucy fell back into the carriage seat and the viscount's passed-out body.

The creature raised its clawed hand, curved steel fingertips glinted in the moonlight. It gripped the man's helmet, and slowly pulled it off, revealing the matted hair and wide trembling, watery eyes of the marquess.

The caped-nobleman whimpered, "I'm sorry for my life of decadence and exploitation. Kill me not. I need to live. I'll never have another libation, no more lecherous delights... no more..."

The creature tossed the helmet aside where it hit the road with a thunk. Lucy saw where the creature's hand had pressed deeply into the bronze.

Lucy wanted to delight in the tables being turned on the mad marquess, but the terror in his voice mirrored her own, and the sight before her would forever haunt her nightmares.

Spring-Heeled Jack hissed, "You're as evil as I." The creature backhanded the marquess. The marquess fell from the wall and crashed onto the muddy road. "Pitiful doppelganger. I should kill you for being a bad me, but letting you live is far more depraved." A sinister little giggle escaped its wicked charcoal lips.

Steam clouds shot out of its calves as Spring-Heeled Jack leapt into the night. Backlit by the moon, demonic laughter reverberated across the countryside.

Lucy sprang to the driver's perch and seized the reins. She turned as the marquess rose. One gauntlet slipped from his trembling hand. He sobbed as the shattered mechanics of his boots fell off with a clatter. Standing, she cracked the leather with a thwap, and the horse's hooves struck the ground. The carriage lurched, smacking the marquess into the mud as she clattered down the road.

The Third Marquess of Waterford was one
of the leading suspects to be the menacing scourge,
Spring-Heeled Jack. In 1846, he suddenly renounced his
lecherous ways, married later that year, and settled into
his estate. The creature known as Spring-Heeled Jack
attacked English travelers for the next century.

The End

Man at the Crossroads

Flash fiction, published in the St. Louis Writers Guild 100th Anniversary Members Anthology

I sat at a dusty crossroads waiting for whatever came my way. Fate was taking a little longer than usual that day. The world shifted out of focus and blurred my vision. Then strolling along the western road, the Devil walked on a mission. A perfect waist and impeccable taste. He's the type people rush online to rate, like a lawyer your mother wants you to date.

Draped in the finest silk suit style, he reached out his bronzed hand with a shiny smile. I shook it out of courtesy because my mother taught me right, but when he tried to yank my soul, I pulled him in real tight. "What is it you need? Why intercede?"

"I'm here for your soul. No loophole."

"You can't feed my greed. You'll never succeed."

"It's dreams I adore. I come bearing contracts, money, and more."

Suddenly surrounded, every fan astounded. Each with a book from my mind awaiting to be signed.

Everything I ever wanted… the vision left me haunted.

"My soul you will not reap. For undaunted, I will not sleep until you realize… my price is not cheap."

He challenged me with a test that sounded bizarre – to rock the greatest song on the electric guitar. I shrugged and said, "no way. I can't even play."

He asked if I could fiddle, and I said, "not even a little."

He challenged me to sing a tune unrehearsed, but my voice was harsh from thirst. A tribute song would sound wrong, so I told him to go away, for a year and a day. He did not play along and crossed his arms to prove he's strong.

The Devil wanted to devour my soul, but I refused his every toll. An explosion of fiery lies burned within his eyes. I caught that horned demon studying me, with a wicked grin he thought I didn't see.

"I challenge you to write the greatest tale ever told." He announced by reading a scroll.

I looked him square in one eye and asked, "Poetry or prose?"

"Either," he said as if loving my woes.

And with a sweet angelic tone, I asked, "word count?"

"Keep it short," he sneered as if tallying the amount.

I wrote until my fingers began to cry and used my blood when the pen went dry. Every word laid down in perfect order, no editor need horde over.

With confidence, I handed him a page of allegory, a one-of-a-kind short story.

His beady eyes align, darting over each line, pondering every word like a fine wine, as if studying a tome at an ancient shrine. The Devil read it thrice times nine, and growled, "You had help from the divine!"

He cast the paper to the ground, which cracked, and fire rose all around. Without a word, he did retract, by covering himself in a shroud of black. He disappeared in a mini mushroom cloud, and I picked up the paper to read the words aloud. "I sat at a dusty crossroads…"

Acknowledgements

Thank you to everyone who encouraged me when they read these stories. Many of them were written when I starting out as a writer, and the encouragement I received allowed me to reach where I am now.

As always, thank you to my critique group, fellow authors who have improved my writing over the years and certainly helped on several of these stories, if not all of them. Cole Gibsen who is not only an amazing author but also doing such great work with her company Got Your Six Support Dogs. T. W. Fendley who is not only one of the best writers I know, but gives so much to others, especially with SLWG. Jennifer Lynn who is a deeply spiritual author and healer, who undoubtably makes me so much better as a writer and a person. Read their books and follow them on social media.

I must mention St. Louis Writers Guild, as much as I might give to others, I have received the same back threefold. I wouldn't be where I am without all my friends and fellow writers in the Guild.

To the Steampunkers! Many thanks for all your support and encouragement and for keeping Steampunk so popular in the world. I write steampunk because I love history and early technology. I'm fascinated by what could have been, and much of that is inspired by the amazing creations we all come up with.

To my wife Amber, for supporting my words and my love of the historical. And for never minding when I hijack out vacations to see something from the past.

Now for a bit about why I wrote each of the stories.

The Baroness

I first wrote this story back in 2010. I entered it in Archon's short story contest where one of the judges, New York Times Bestselling Author Angie Fox, read it and liked it. She gave me some great advice about stretching out the moment and told me I had something with this character. She was right. The story would go on to place in a couple of contests. When I decided to write Iron Horsemen, this story and airships firing broadsides in the sky, ignited a flame that became The Iron Chronicles.

To anyone who reads my novels, the feel of those books is much more hopeful. I was experimenting with mood when I wrote this. Plus, this story is not canon, yet, but you can see the seeds of the trilogy are all here in this story. Maybe one day, I'll get to write the Genevieve Demon Slayer series, but for now, I'm happy to share this tale with you.

Touch the Stars

I've been a fan of Jules Verne since I was young, he is one of the reasons I write Steampunk, and I wanted to pay tribute to him, and movies like The Explorers, where anybody could reach space with a lot of imagination and some scientific know-how. As a former Ferret owner, I wanted to include one to honor my George. My friend and fellow writer, Ronald R Van Stockum Jr. is a fellow Vernian and we have held workshops on his writing and the technology he incorporated.

Doomed Flight of the Majestic

The inspiration for this story came after the death of Robert Osborne. For years, I watched him host all my favorite classic movies on TCM (Turner Classic Movies). As a tribute to him, I wrote a piece and thought about him telling some of the great behind-the-scenes stories. I tried to tell a story where the backstory was better than the movie itself. Thank you, Robert Osborne for the Master Class in Hollywood's Golden Age. I love old movies and this story is an homage to those amazing cinematic adventures. I was also wanting to touch on Dieselpunk as I mostly write Steampunk.

A Clockwork Heart

I wrote A Clockwork Heart many years ago, I'm usually an upbeat writer of adventure stories, but this allowed me to write something more touching but still clad in Steampunk. This story has been widely loved placing in several contest, and has been one of my bestselling stories since it was published.

The Legend of Spring-Heeled Jack

The Legend of Spring-Heeled Jack came from a real myth I was reading one day. Instantly the thought of a steampunk demon came to mind and I had to write it down. I tried for a couple of years to release the story on Halloween but other projects always took precident. It is my story of the true creature and a possible reason the nobleman changed his ways.

Man at the Crossroads

Man at the Crossroads was one of the first things I wrote, but I never did anything with it until I needed a piece for the St. Louis Writers Guild 100th Anniversary Members Anthology. It reflects a style of writing that I enjoy but so rarely get to play with. To play with words and have fun with stories.

More Stories from
Brad R. Cook

Novels
The Iron Chronicles
Iron Horesemen, Iron Zulu, & Iron Lotus

Steamtree: The Airdrainium Adventures

The History of St. Louis Writers Guild
Celebrating a Century

Short Stories
The Secret of Knotbridge Hill
The Dragon Slayer
Tales of the Gearblade

Anthologies
Out of Darkness Vol. II
St. Louis Reflections
Love Letters to St. Louis
St. Louis Writers Guild 100th Anniversary
Members Anthology

About the Author

Brad R. Cook
Author and Historian
I see things that never were and say, "Why not?"

Brad R. Cook, is the author of historical fantasy, and award-winning short stories. He began as a playwright, dipped into the corporate writing world, and served as co-publisher and acquisitions editor for Blank Slate Press. He currently serves as Historian of St. Louis Writers Guild after three and half years as President. He learned to fence at thirteen, and never set down his sword, but prefers to curl up with a centuries' old classic.

@bradrcook
bradrcook.com